I0662701

Doggone Ugly Creek

by

Cheryel Hutton

Ugly Creek Series, Book 3

This is a work of fiction. Names, characters, places, and incidents are either the product of the author's imagination or are used fictitiously, and any resemblance to actual persons living or dead, business establishments, events, or locales, is entirely coincidental.

Doggone Ugly Creek

COPYRIGHT © 2017 by Cheryel Hutton

All rights reserved. No part of this book may be used or reproduced in any manner whatsoever without written permission of the author or The Wild Rose Press, Inc. except in the case of brief quotations embodied in critical articles or reviews.
Contact Information: info@thewildrosepress.com

Cover Art by *Debbie Taylor*

The Wild Rose Press, Inc.
PO Box 708
Adams Basin, NY 14410-0708
Visit us at www.thewildrosepress.com

Publishing History
First Fantasy Rose Edition, 2017
Print ISBN 978-1-5092-1254-5
Digital ISBN 978-1-5092-1255-2

Ugly Creek Series, Book 3
Published in the United States of America

Stop, my brain cried out. Back away from the lunatic! Instead, my rebellious arms slid around his neck, finding muscles I didn't realize he had. My fingers touched him like his skin was Braille, and I was hungry to read his story.

His hands spread over my back and he pulled me close. It felt good to be held. To be warm and secure in the strong arms of a man. Even if they were part of an annoying guy who cared more about dogs than the people around him. That's me, no-life Shay.

I shoved him away. "What the hell do you think you're doing?"

"Me?" His face went red and the muscles in his cheeks and around his eyes tightened. "You're the one who kissed *me*."

"Don't blame me, you're the one who started that kiss."

Ace's shoulders dropped and he closed his eyes for a moment. "We kissed each other."

"Crap." He was right, it had been a mutual touching of lips. My fingers, the same ones that had just caressed Ace's neck and shoulders, touched my still tingling lips as I wondered what had just happened.

"Was it that bad?" His lips were pulled into a crooked little grin.

Dedication

To all the dedicated people
who spend so much of their time and money
to save animals from situations of abuse or neglect.
You are all heroes!

Chapter 1

Ugly Creek was the prettiest little town I'd ever seen. Almost unnaturally clean and neat, it was also quiet and friendly. Not a bad place to start over.

I was on my knees, on the front lawn of my Aunt Ruth's little white house, pulling a few weeds that had dared to grow among the irises in her gorgeous flower garden. I promised myself I would keep her pride and joy as nice as possible. I can usually hold my own with plants, but nobody does flowers like my aunt. I think she could probably grow prize-winning roses out of a rock.

A large collie pushed open the front door and bounded off the porch.

I grinned at the beast. "I wondered how long it would take for you to decide to come out and play."

The collie gave me a doggie smile, then proceeded to lope around the corner of the house.

This starting over thing might not be so bad after all.

Just then a huge dog that looked like a mix of Great Dane and Lab leaped over the white picket fence and headed straight for our backyard.

"Watch out!" I yelled.

Before I could get to my feet and follow the dog, a human interloper rushed through the front gate. He stopped to shut and latch the gate before he ran toward the backyard—without even glancing my way.

I took off running, sliding to a stop near where he was standing. At the back of the house, the collie and the rich chocolate colored dog were sniffing each other's hindquarters. "That's disgusting."

"Sniffing each other's rears is a perfectly natural way for dogs to get to know each other."

The voice was surprisingly deep and rich for a guy whose sun-bleached hair and tan reminded me of a beach bum .

I eyed the trespasser. "And who the hell are you?"

He held out his hand. "Ace Ellison, and you must be Shay. Shay Carpenter, right?"

I kept my hands where they were. "How could you possibly know who I am?"

"I know your aunt." He smiled. "Ruth's a fascinating person."

I ignored his on-the-nose assessment of my eccentric, aunt who loved horror movies and wore bright purple, blue, and red clothes. Instead, I met his gaze and held it. "I suppose that's your dog over there."

He dropped his hand. "Sort of."

"Sort of?" I crossed my arms in front of me and glared hard. His eyes were sort of greenish something that seemed to change color when he moved. Like a chameleon. Figures.

"He's a rescue."

"Rescued from what?"

His T-shirt and faded jeans fit snugly, setting off flat abs. He crossed his arms over those abs. "Hugh here was rescued from an irresponsible owner, but we rescue dogs from all kinds of bad situations."

Hugh? "Like that TV show about the guy who

rescues pit bulls?"

The frown that pulled above his full eyebrows and the frustration I saw in his eyes lightened my mood considerably.

"Pretty much," he said. "Except I rescue all breeds of dog, and sometimes other animals."

"On television I've seen rescuers break into places to get dogs out."

He held my gaze, his full lips tightening.

"Rescuers don't like to see animals abused. Sometimes it's a judgment call how far to go to protect them."

Judgment call, huh? I didn't like this guy. His attitude needed adjusting. Movement caught my gaze, and I saw the dogs running together and playing like puppies. "He's a rescue? Are you sure he doesn't have a disease or fleas or something?" From the corner of my eye, I saw him glare at me.

"I'd hate for your dog to get rescue fleas."

"Her," I said, without acknowledging his sarcastic tone. "The collie's a girl."

"Come on, Hugh. We need to get you back where you belong." He started toward the dog, who immediately took off in another direction, followed closely by the collie.

"Trixie, come here," I said, trying to catch the eye of the errant dog.

He turned from his chase to look at me. "*Trixie?* Really?"

I turned my gaze on him again. His sun-bleached sandy blond hair was mussed like he'd just emerged from bed. Sexy. Not that I cared. "What's wrong with Trixie? No worse than Hugh."

"Just kinda old-fashioned." He shrugged. "I didn't name Hugh."

"I didn't name Trixie either. She's my cousin's dog." I gave him a good glare. "Not that there's anything wrong with that name."

Ace headed toward Hugh, who gave him a look and took off in another direction. I barely held back laughter as man and dog did a little dance around each other. Ace, with some type of red rope at the ready, kept at the effort longer than I would have. That man must have serious patience. Dang, I wish he'd hurry up. It was getting hot out here in the sun. Watching a well-built male body had nothing to do with it. Really.

When Ace finally cornered the dog near the back porch, I breathed a sigh of relief. He deftly slipped a loop of rope over Hugh's neck, and tightened it. Hugh, seeming to concede defeat, sat on the ground.

"Come on, boy." Ace tugged the rope, and Hugh went with him.

Relief filled me as I watched the two head toward the front gate. Before he went through, Ace gave me a big smile, and a wave. "Later."

Anger sent heat through my body as I watched the man take his dog down the street. He looked good from the back, I conceded. He had broad shoulders and a well-shaped rear. Hey, just because I disliked the man didn't mean I couldn't enjoy the scenery.

I pulled my T-shirt collar out to allow in a bit of air. The temperature must be rising fast. I didn't see Trixie, so I started toward the front. The air conditioner in the house would be more than welcome right now.

"You know that Ellison boy?" a woman's voice asked.

I turned toward the waist-high, white fence between our yard and the next. A medium-height, silver-haired woman wearing a lime green dress stood there. Her face carried some signs of aging, but not as wrinkled as a person would expect from someone with gray hair.

I walked toward her. "No, we just met."

"You're Ruth's niece, aren't you?"

"Yes, I'm Shay."

"I'm Camilla Carlisle. It's nice to meet you. I've known that aunt of yours for years."

"It's nice to meet you too." There was something about the woman that bothered me. Maybe it was that she seemed to look down her nose at me. Or the feeling she enjoyed inserting her opinion into things that didn't concern her. Whatever the clue my subconscious had picked up on, I wasn't convinced she was really the sweet little old lady she appeared to be.

"I believe Ruth would want me to look out for you."

Our new neighbor shook her head and tightened her thin mouth.

"You watch out, you hear me. That Ellison boy is trouble."

I quite agreed, but more info is never a bad idea. "Is he?"

"Absolutely. He's got about a hundred dogs, you know. Mutts and strays all of them."

"He said he's an animal rescuer of some kind."

The woman snorted. "He's a blight on our beautiful community, that's what he is. Nobody ought to be allowed to have a bunch of animals right in town. Hordes of nasty beasts belong on a farm."

"Where does he live?"

She pointed in the direction I'd seen him go.

"That-a-way and over two streets. His place is at the end of the road and down a hill, but I can still hear his mutts all times of the day and night." She sighed. "And I don't hear as good as I used to."

I smiled. "I'll steer clear of Ace."

She gave a quick punctuating nod. "Good for you. Now I need to get back inside before I melt. It's hot for September."

Miz Carlisle went toward her house, and I turned toward the place that would be my home for a year, or at least that was the plan. I grabbed the gloves I'd been using to pull weeds and headed toward the front porch. "Come on, Trixie! We've got work to do."

Trixie let out a little whimper, then followed me inside.

I put the gloves on one of the shelves attached to the wall near the back door. Aunt Ruth kept all her gardening things neatly organized, which definitely made it easier for me.

I then turned back to the totally unorganized pile of boxes in the living room. For two single women who lived with their mothers, my cousin and I had a lot of stuff, and apparently we'd brought most of it with us.

"Don't trust that Carlisle woman."

I turned in time to see my cousin pulling on her shirt. At least she was getting dressed, which wasn't always a sure thing. "What are you talking about, Terri? She seems like a nice old lady who's concerned about her friend's niece."

Terri rolled her eyes. "Leave it to my cousin to see good in everybody."

She headed toward the kitchen, and I went after her. "You don't like her, I take it?"

Terri stuck her head in the fridge and rooted around. "She's a mean old broad, and her cat's the spawn of Satan."

I bit back the grin. "Well, it's understandable that you wouldn't like cats."

She turned back out of the fridge, her arms full of turkey, two kinds of cheese, mustard, mayo, tomato, lettuce, and pickles. I had no idea how she managed to get them to the table. If I tried that, I'd have a big mess to clean up.

"I like cats," she said. "Why would you think I wouldn't?"

"Because you're…well, you're a dog. Or at least part of the time you are."

Her shoulders shook so hard with laughter she had to pause in her food preparation. "Dogs like cats. At least some of them do."

"Yeah, to chase."

Terri shook her head. "Dogs are as diverse as humans, just so you know."

I studied her face. "So you really like cats, except the demon spawn ones?"

"Yes, and don't be so weird about me being a shifter. You've known me your whole life." She shoved a couple of slices of turkey into her mouth.

I sighed. "It just feels odd, you and me living here for a year. Honestly, I'm not always sure how to handle being around you."

She grinned and patted my face.

"Just love me."

"You know I do."

She shoved the fixings back into the fridge and took the huge sandwich with her toward her bedroom. Hopefully to unpack boxes. "Let me know what you want to do about dinner."

I leaned against the counter, laughing and shaking my head in amazement. Terri could eat like a growing male teenager, something about using so much energy to shift between woman and collie. My cousin, the bestselling author. And dog.

I didn't know whether to laugh or cry. All I knew was that the next few months promised to be anything but dull.

Chapter 2

Loud, pounding music blasted me out of a sweet dream. A glance at the clock told me it was still a good three hours before sunrise. Groaning, I slid out of bed and stumbled toward the other bedroom.

Terri sat at her desk, her hands flying over a laptop keyboard while her body swayed to the beat of what I vaguely recognized as an old AC/DC song. I took a moment to rein in the seething heat in my belly. She was my cousin; I couldn't strangle her. Right?

"What the hell do you think you're doing?" I yelled so she could hear me.

"I'm writing," she yelled back without so much as a glance in my direction.

I clicked off the stereo. Terri spun her chair and glared at me like I'd just killed her new puppy.

"Why did you do that? I was on a roll."

I crossed my arms and glared back. "I was asleep."

She opened her mouth and held it for a moment, then closed it as she leaned back in her chair. "I'm sorry. I'm used to writing in the morning and I always write to music."

"There's a new invention," I told her. "Headphones."

She poked out her bottom lip. "But those can damage your hearing."

"Loud music can damage your hearing no matter

how you listen to it. Waking up your cousin in the middle of the night isn't conducive to good health either."

"It's not the middle of the night, it's almost four."

"Like I said, middle of the night."

Her mouth pulled to one side as she shuffled over to her closet, where she pulled out a nice pair of big, neon green headphones. "All right. I'll put these on."

"Thank you." I turned to go back to bed.

"You know, early morning is a very productive time to write. You should try it."

I took a moment to count to one hundred, just so I wouldn't need somebody to bail me out of the Ugly Creek jail. My cousin was the only one I really knew in town, and she probably wouldn't want to come get me if I'd just tried to kill her.

I tried reasoning with her. "Terri, four o'clock is not morning, it's the middle of the damn night."

She shrugged. "Rising early works for a lot of very successful writers. So does writing to music. For instance, Stephen King writes to loud music."

I glared so hard my vision went blurry. "I write at night, when it's quiet, like a lot of very successful writers. You know as well as I do, every writer has to do what works best for them." With that, I turned and stomped back to bed.

I hoped sleep would quickly return, but it was not to be. My thoughts swirled round and round. Terri was irresponsible. Aunt Ruth wanted the two of us to stay here while she traveled, saying that Terri and I needed an opportunity to get to know each other better.

I loved my cousin. I enjoyed being with her. I loved her goofy sense of humor. It was true we hadn't seen each other for any length of time since we were kids. Mostly we got together on the rushed days during holidays. We all knew Terri tended to be more than a little free-spirited. Aunt Ruth confided in me once that Terri's mother, my aunt, still had to keep an eye on her twenty-eight year-old daughter.

It was bad enough that she acted first and thought later, but she didn't seem to understand how serious protecting her secret really was. For all I knew, Aunt Ruth might have wanted the two of us to stay here in her house so that I could keep an eye on Terri and her secret identity while her mom was away.

It made sense, I guess. Terri was almost two years older than me, but Mom's illness had made me the caretaker of the family. Thing was, I was tired of being responsible for another person. I'd taken care of my mom since I was barely a teenager. I'd hoped this year would be my introduction to a life of freedom.

A little after four, I rose and pulled out my laptop. If I couldn't sleep, at least maybe I could make some progress on my latest manuscript.

****

By nine, I was dressed in black jeans, comfortable black ballet flats, and a cute sea-green short-sleeved blouse that went well with my red hair. I hoped I looked like a reasonable facsimile of a reporter as I walked into the downtown office of the twice-weekly *Ugly Creek Gazette*.

The place opened off Market Street, near the corner of Main where the courthouse was located. The inside walls were painted beige, but were almost completely papered with front pages from years of the little newspaper. I could have happily spent the next few days perusing the headlines and reading the articles.

A long table ran almost the entire left wall, and along the right were three basic wooden desks. Papers were strewn over all three desks, along with empty coffee mugs and various papers, writing implements, desktop computers a few years old, and rectangular cleared spaces the size of laptops. Nobody currently sat at any of them. Toward the back, an open door likely led to the editor's office.

A tall man, high cheekbones, salt-and-pepper hair, and a few wrinkles to complete the distinguished face came out that door to greet me. "Good morning, Ms. Carpenter, I'm Fred Costa. It's good to have you with us."

"Thank you, sir."

His smile of welcome seemed sincere, but there was a glimmer of concern in his brown eyes. "I have a job for you."

Oh boy. "What sort of job?"

"Animal Services is gearing up to remove a hoard of cats from an old woman's home. I want you and a photographer to head over there and see if you can't get a human angle on the raid. Miz Funderburk is an odd one but if you can convince her to talk to you it should be an interesting story."

I wondered if I was being suckered into a crazy story as a test, when I remembered how small Ugly Creek was. This kind of event was newsworthy when nothing major was happening. Which was probably most of the time.

"No problem."

The concern in his eyes vanished. "Good, there's your photographer now."

I turned and Ace Ellison's gaze met mine. Perfect. Absolutely freaking perfect.

A smirk twitched at his lips. "We can take my car."

When pigs went snorkeling. "I'll meet you there."

I spun and headed out the door and into the sweet "candy blue" Ford Focus I'd saved for three years to pay cash for so I could stay out of debt. I dug around in my purse and twiddled my toes until Ace disappeared down the road. Then I called Mr. Costa to get the address. I expected irritation from my boss, but what I got sounded a lot like amusement.

That Ace dude was going to drive me totally avocadoes—or maybe even kumquats.

Five minutes later I pulled in behind Ace's big, dark gray, what was that thing? I squinted in the sunlight to see the little silver letters on the back. Xterra. Why in the world would a single man in his twenties need a vehicle that big? Was he compensating for something? Hmm, made sense to me.

As soon as I parked, he popped out of his behemoth—okay, maybe it wasn't *that* big—and was beside my car before I could get out.

"What took you so long?"

"I did my nails."

He rolled his eyes and tipped his head toward the rough looking two-story house. The paint was peeling, the porch sagged, and the roof probably let in half the rain that fell on it.

"This is the place," Ace said, and headed toward said place.

I groaned. "Figures."

I caught up with him about the time he reached the porch, just before he knocked. I'd have been happy to stand back and wait for the animal shelter people, but I wasn't about to let the likes of Ace Ellison outdo me. I carefully climbed the squeaky steps, and got to Ace just as an elderly woman pulled open the door. The odor of cat urine and decay billowed over us, and it took an effort to keep my breakfast where it belonged.

"Can I help you?"

The voice had an edge that told me she'd love to help us go away.

I put on my best smile and held out my hand. "Miz Funderburk, my name is Shay Carpenter. I'm a reporter for the *Ugly Creek Gazette*. Would it be okay if I asked you some questions?"

The woman narrowed her eyes at me.

"This is about my cats, isn't it? Nobody's taking my babies from me."

Ace stepped around me and positioned himself closer to the woman. "We don't want to take your cats. Actually, we'd like to tell your side of the story."

She still had an expression of distrust, but she seemed to be less ready to slam the door in our faces.

"My side?"

"Yes," I jumped in, shoving the irritating man aside as I did. "We're interested in your love for animals."

Miz Funderburk's eyes glistened and her chin trembled. "My cats aren't animals to me, they're my children."

From the smells coming from the house, she didn't treat her "children" very well. Apparently trying to escape, three of those kitty kids shoved past her and out onto the porch. An orange tabby and an extremely skinny black-and-white cat rushed toward the end of the porch. Gracefully, they jumped off into the yard. The smaller cat, gray or maybe even white, I couldn't tell, rubbed against my legs. The little thing's fur was matted and nasty. It was all I could do not to gag at the thought of what the cat was depositing on my new black jeans. At least I hadn't worn a skirt.

"How adorable," I managed. It would be if it wasn't covered in trash.

The woman smiled. "He's a cutie."

There was a sound from the road and I glanced over my shoulder to check it out. I barely caught a glimpse of the animal control vehicle when Miz Funderburk screamed.

I looked, and she was shaking her fists at us. "You lying scum. You're in with them! You aren't taking my babies!" She moved to slam the door.

Ace had his body in the way and his foot against the door. "We have nothing to do with them. We want to tell your story."

"I don't believe you." She shoved at Ace, and he stumbled back. The door slammed shut so hard the floorboards of the porch vibrated.

The cat at my feet shot off the porch and disappeared. I turned to see two guys coming from the animal control truck. I wanted to be anywhere but there when they tried to make her open that door. There's no way they could force her, right? At least not without police and some sort of official order.

A red convertible with its top down swung around the animal control vehicle and came to a screeching stop. A woman dressed in a gray business suit and beat-up athletic shoes slid out of the car and marched across the yard. She gave us a smoldering glare as she went to the door and knocked. "Mom, open the door."

"Go away!"

"Mom." There was pain in the new arrival's voice. "Please, I only want to help you."

"Taking my babies isn't helping me."

Two police cars, one local Ugly Creek and one county sheriff, pulled off the road. The two uniformed policemen got out of their cruisers and headed toward the house. The two men from the animal shelter, each carrying two portable cages, joined them.

"We'd better get out of the way."

Ace grabbed my arm and tugged.

My first instinct was to resist, but then I considered just how packed the porch was about to be. Not to mention what was about to happen.

We barely got down the steps before the group reached us. The cops continued up the steps, but one of the animal shelter dudes stepped directly in front of Ace.

"I'm watching you, Ellison." Loathing dripped from the man's words.

Ace met the man's gaze. "I'm well aware, Vanetti."

Vanetti glared for a moment longer, then rejoined his fellow animal shelter dude who was pointedly ignoring his buddy and Ace.

The animal guys went up the steps, taking a position to the side and near the cops. The porch wasn't small, still the five of them created a formidable mass in front of the door. I cringed at the thought of what was going through the mind of the woman inside. In the piece for the paper, I planned to try to capture what had to be a feeling of panic and betrayal. I had seen so many TV news shows about animal hoarders and thought how wonderful it was when the authorities stepped in to rescue the poor creatures, but I'd never, ever thought about the toll that rescue took on the hoarder herself.

As I considered my new insight, I saw the daughter put a key in the lock and shove the door inward. The effort was stopped by something, or someone, from the inside of the house blocking the door.

"Let me in, Mom," the daughter said.

"You're not taking my babies," Miz Funderburk told her.

"Mom, please don't make this harder than it has to be."

I watched the unfolding scene with mounting horror. This would not end well, and I was bound by contract to report what happened.

"You wouldn't let anybody take away your children." Miz Funderburk's voice was getting higher pitched by the moment.

"They aren't your children, Mom. They're animals."

"You don't understand. Go away!"

"Mom, the neighbors have complained. You could lose your house. Please don't force me to do this."

"I'm not forcing you to do anything. I'm fine here; Ugly Creek takes care of its own. Go on back home and take care of your own damn business." The door slammed, and I heard the lock click.

The daughter stood with her hands on the door, her head down, her shoulders slumped. "Mom."

The anger in that one word sent chills down my spine.

"This is embarrassing, Mom. Open the door."

Embarrassing? I could think of a lot of words to describe the situation; embarrassing wasn't one of them.

One of the cops took the key from the daughter's hand, and she turned away as the police forced the door in. I could see Miz Funderburk struggling hard to keep the men out, but she didn't stand a chance.

I stood there, a captive observer, while a woman wailed and begged the four men not to take her babies. I'm not the crying type, but I admit to shedding tears as I watched the horrible battle of wills. Miz Funderburk's daughter had taken refuge in her car, where she leaned against the steering wheel. If this was hard for me, I couldn't imagine what it must be like for a daughter. I don't think I would have been strong enough to do what she did.

On the other hand, I do know I would have had more compassion for my mother. For that matter, where had that daughter been all the time this hoarding was going on? Why hadn't she been there helping her mother and letting her know she was loved?

The police held Miz Funderburk out in the front yard. It took one man holding each arm, as she begged and kicked and wrenched trying to free herself.

I saw flashes of light from inside the dark house, flashes I figured were from the camera I'd seen around the less obnoxious animal control officer's neck. They were documenting what they found, I realized. Made sense. They would have to explain in court why they'd done what they did. Which was to break a woman's heart.

Then the two men started bringing carriers out of

the house and Miz Funderburk screamed. If there hadn't been some small movement within the carriers, I'd have thought the cats were dead. As they passed us I got a whiff of the most horrible, nauseating smell I'd ever encountered. They brought out some black plastic garbage bags also, which had to be cats that were dead. Both men were wearing thick gloves and white paper face masks.

One of the cops found Miz Funderburk a chair, and she settled down to a heart-wrenching wail, which I tried hard to ignore as more and more carriers and bags came out. I edged closer to the porch, and caught a glimpse of the inside of the house. I couldn't see much, but it looked like boxes were stacked as high as I could see.

Curious, I boldly moved even closer, and while animal control wasn't looking, I went up the steps and across the porch. The closer I got to the open door, the stronger the smell became. It was the same cat urine and decay as before, but stronger—much stronger. I forced back the gag and stepped into the house.

It was impossible to see more than a foot or so. Boxes, furniture, papers, clothing, and junk were piled higher than my head. There was only a small opening through the stuff, just enough for one person to slide through.

"You just had to see for yourself, didn't you?"

I gasped, which I immediately regretted when the stench burned my lungs. The Vanetti dude stood behind me.

"I'm a reporter," I told him. "I need to see what's going on in order to report."

"Have at it." He tossed me a paper mask attached

to an elastic band, pulled his own up from where it hung around his neck to cover his mouth and nose, then shoved past me through the narrow passage leading farther into the house.

I edged through the pile of everything imaginable behind the man. Houseflies swarmed the place, and the smell was all but overwhelming, but I forced back my reaction and kept on going. I may not exactly be a reporter, but I am a writer, and we are a curious bunch.

The stench worsened as I moved through the maze of garbage. The piles weren't so high in places, and I managed to see across the tops of some. Unfolding through the rooms of what had once been a magnificent home was a landscape of newspapers, boxes of all shapes and sizes, furniture stacked on top of furniture, and garbage of all shapes and colors. It looked like a landfill. Smelled like one too.

The men were doing something to one side, and I craned my neck to see. Then I wished I'd have let my writer self stay curious. They were scooping up the body of a cat, long dead, covered with maggots. Okay, curiosity satisfied. I was quite done, thank you.

Rushing was impossible back through the walls of junk. I tried not to breathe and just keep moving while not touching anything. Even with the paper mask, the smell was awful. It seemed to take forever to retrace the few feet I'd come. I was beginning to think I was actually lost in the maze, and the thought of being trapped in there made my stomach churn again.

I moved around an old, cabinet-style television stacked high with a huge box filled with dolls and plastic containers of something brown and nasty that might have started life as fruits or vegetables. There was clothing, empty milk cartons, frozen food boxes, and things I couldn't begin to identify stacked on top of each other and reaching the ceiling. I thought I recognized some of the stuff as cups and plates, and hung onto that thought as I pushed myself through the next few steps.

There it was. The open door standing before me like the sought-after treasure it was. I swallowed hard and carefully moved closer and closer to the way out.

Once free, I rushed across the porch, stumbled down the front steps, and ran several feet from the house. With one hand, I braced myself against a beautiful walnut tree, its solid hulk supporting my weak and trembling body, its rough bark firm and comforting against my hand. By some miracle I didn't vomit, though it wasn't through my body's lack of trying.

"Here, this will help your stomach."

I looked at Ace, surprised he was beside me, surprised at the cellophane wrapped pink pill, and stunned at the caring in his voice.

"Thank you," I managed. With trembling fingers, I opened the package and shoved the medicine in my mouth.

"You're the reporter, it's your call, but this is going to take hours. We probably have all the info we're going to get."

"You're saying we should leave?"

Ace shrugged. "Like I said, it's up to you, but I think the party's over."

"You've been to a lot of animal hoarder things?"

"A few."

Something in his voice, something deep and painful, had me looking at his face. His eyes were dark and haunted, and I could see fine lines at the corners. Lines he was far too young to have.

"Are they always this bad?" I wasn't sure I wanted to know.

"Usually they're worse." He turned and strode back toward the front of the house.

He was right; we had what we came for. I headed the way he'd gone, giving him a "let's go" motion as I passed. The relief in his eyes was evident.

I headed home toward a two-hour shower, the face of poor Miz Funderburk haunting me the whole way.

Chapter 3

I woke the next morning to the blessed sound of quiet. Terri had listened and remembered. Let me tell you, I was amazed. I'd have to do something nice for her.

Jeans and a T-shirt, five minutes in the bathroom, and I was ready to take on the day. At least I hoped I was. Yesterday's cat lady adventure had shaken me more than I wanted to admit.

The remains of Terri's morning cup of tea were on the counter by the sink. She loves the stuff, but I need something with more caffeine or I won't make it to lunch. So I put on a pot of coffee.

I had my head in the fridge, reaching for my yummy hazelnut coffee creamer, when I heard the doggy door open. I straightened up to find Terri standing naked two feet from me.

"It's great outside," she said, as she pushed me aside in order to grab a bottle of water from the fridge.

I was used to Terri's complete lack of modesty, but I doubted I'd ever be comfortable with it. Not to mention the slight lingering scent of dog always weirded me out. "Thanks for being quiet this morning."

"You're welcome," she said.

I sipped at my coffee, while Terri pulled out bread, mustard, and lunch meat. "Want a sandwich?"

"Too early."

"It's almost eleven." The look on her face was one of total confusion.

"I was up late last night."

She shrugged as if the whole idea was foreign to her. "We've been invited to a barbeque tonight."

I carefully swallowed the hot liquid in my mouth. "A what?"

"Barbeque. Cookout. The thing where meat is cooked over hot coals."

I chose to ignore her bait. "We haven't lived here a week yet, how did we manage to get invited to anything?"

Terri shrugged. "A nice lady came by. She's a friend of Aunt Ruth's, and she said she wanted to welcome us to the neighborhood. "

I groaned. "Let me guess, she's a hundred-and-six, has gray-blue hair, and uses a walker."

"You'd be wrong." Terri bit off a big bite and spoke around the food. "Her name's Lily Bennett, and she's young, about your age."

"Not old like you?"

Terri chuckled. "Just call me Granny."

I am, for the record, all of two years younger than my twenty-eight year old cousin. "What time is this shindig?"

"Starts at six."

"You gonna wear clothes?"

"Smartass." She sucked down the rest of the sandwich and water then headed for the back door, shifting as she went

"It was a legitimate question," I told the collie. She gave me a sharp little bark, then slipped through the doggy door.

I poured some warm coffee into the cooling liquid in my cup, then leaned against the counter and considered this living with my cousin thing. I might just be in over my head.

****

Lily and Ken Bennett's house was a cute yellow bungalow over three streets and near the neighborhood's main road. The couple greeted us warmly while the aroma of meat cooking on the nearby grill had my mouth watering. I glanced toward Terri and saw her nose twitch. I sent up a little request that she not do something crazy like grab a piece of meat off the grill and scarf it down in a couple of huge bites. And yes, she was fully capable of doing just that.

Lily's husband Ken greeted us, then headed back to the food while Lily took us over to meet the other guests.

"This is Stephie and Jake," Lily said. "Guys, meet Shay and Terri."

I smiled and shook hands, all the while trying to place the man.

He got there first. "You're the impromptu ballerina from that Fourth of July celebration a few years back."

My face went hot and I swallowed hard. "Oh no, you probably think I'm a nut."

"Hardly." Jake glanced toward Stephie. "It was about fifteen years ago. There was this adorable girl who suddenly broke into a ballet dance right on the courthouse lawn. Even at my age, I could tell she had amazing talent." He glanced at me and grinned. "And obviously a drive to perform."

"Oh! I hope you followed that dream," Stephie smiled, her eyes shiny and hopeful.

I wanted to run back to the house as fast as I could, throw myself on my bed, and cry until I couldn't cry anymore. Instead, I pulled up my big girl panties and forced my lips into a smile. "Actually, things just didn't work out that way. Instead I became a writer."

"What do you write?" she asked.

I felt my face go hot. Talking about myself was not something I enjoyed. "Mostly novels, plus some freelance journalism to help pay the bills." I grabbed my cousin's arm and pulled her closer. "Terri's the one who kicks butt. How many times have you been on the *New York Times*'s bestseller list?"

"Four, but you're an amazing writer, Shay." Terri leaned a bit closer to her audience. "She writes as Shannon Alexis. Check out her books, they're great."

Stephie, Jake, and Lily all looked excited and promised to check out both our literary accomplishments. I looked at my cousin and silently tried to convey how grateful I was for her help. She gave me a one-armed hug as she told them about my contemporary romances and her urban fantasies. They looked appropriately impressed, and I slid into the familiar, but still kind of amazing, role of almost-semi-famous-local-author. I was fine as long as I didn't have to toot my own horn.

Lily greeted her newly arrived guest. "Hello, Ace. Glad you could make it."

"Thank you for inviting me." Ace gave Lily a quick hug.

"Have you met our new neighbors Terri and Shay?"

He smiled. "Hello, Shay."

"Ace."

26

Terri bounced over to him, wiggling all over. "Hi, Ace. You have an awesome dog."

"You'll have to be more specific." He grinned. "I have quite a few."

"Hugh." She wiggled some more. "He's fun."

A frown pulled at Ace's forehead. "How do you know Hugh?"

"I saw him out the window when you came by Aunt Ruth's house the other day."

Skepticism clouded his features, and I totally understood.

"I didn't know anyone other than Shay was home," he said.

"I was unpacking," she told him.

I gave her a serious glare, but she ignored me.

"Well, it's nice to meet you, Terri. You're welcome to come by and see Hugh anytime."

"Feel free to bring him to our house whenever you like. I know Trixie loves playing with him."

"Thank you. Hugh definitely enjoyed playing with her."

The two of them smiled at each other. Now that was a weird pair. I guess it made an odd sort of sense, the dog lover and the dog. I faked a cough to cover my laugh.

"I just realized I read one of your books a few months ago."

I smiled at Stephie. "Good to know somebody has."

"I loved the book, but I read it just before I met Jake." She laughed softly as her face reddened. "I planned to read more of your work, but I got a bit distracted."

I glanced toward her handsome husband. "I can see how that could happen. Who needs a book when you've got a real-life romance going on?"

Her eyes lit up as she smiled. "Me. I love Jake, but I need my romance novel fix. "Now that I remember how good that book was, I can't wait to read more."

"Thank you." My face was hot. "I hope you like whichever you choose."

"Well, look what the cat dragged in," a female voice said.

Stephie and I both looked toward the tiny, blonde woman who Ace had turned to meet with a hug.

"That's Liza," Stephie told me. "She's an interesting person, and a great friend."

I smiled, wondering what it would be like to have all these nice folks as friends. With the exception of Ace, of course.

A man wearing wire-framed glasses wrapped his arms around Liza and pulled her against him. "Hands off my wife, Ellison."

Ace backed away, his hands up in mock surrender.

Liza smacked her husband on the arm. "Stop acting like a caveman, Steve."

The caveman rolled his eyes and held out his hand. "Good to see you, Ace. How's it going?"

"Same as usual. Most people around here are great, but the few who aren't are a big pain in the ass."

"Let me know if you need anything."

"Thanks, buddy."

The two bumped fists, then jumped into a lively discussion of the Tennessee Volunteers versus the Georgia Bulldogs college football teams.

Liza groaned and turned away. That's when she

spotted Terri and me. "You must be Ruth Capps's nieces. I'm Liza and that geeky caveman over there is my husband, Steve."

"Shay," I said, extending my hand. "From what I've seen, the other one's pretty primitive too."

She glanced over her shoulder before taking my hand. "Aren't all men?"

"Sadly, I believe they might be."

"Hi, I'm Terri."

Liza took the offered hand. "Hi, Terri. Nice to meet you."

"You and your husband own Z-Com Tech, right?"

"Yes we do. How in the world did you know that?"

"I did a lot of research for a book I wrote. Software tech is fascinating stuff."

Terri and Liza bonded over tech talk until Lily announced the food was ready. I got myself a steak and salad, then took my plate and drink and sat them on the edge of a small table near the periphery. There was an available chair nearby, but I wanted to stand so I could mingle or move, whichever I needed.

"Hiding in the corner, huh?"

Stephie sat her food on the table near mine.

"My kind of party goer."

I smiled. "Good to discover a kindred soul."

"Supposedly, artistic types tend to be introverts, so I guess we fit the profile."

I racked my brain for what I'd heard she did. "You're a photographer, right?"

She nodded. "And I help Jake at the antique shop."

"Doesn't that involve working with people?"

She let out a big, heartfelt sigh. "Yes, it does, but I love our inventory. I also love helping Jake. Who is extroverted, of course. Along with both Madison and Liza, my two closest friends."

I nodded my understanding. "Terri is too," I told her. We both looked toward my cousin, who seemed to be having the time of her life right in the midst of the partygoers.

She grinned. "I guess we'll have to hold down the introvert end of the group."

"I guess we will."

There was a friendly connection between us that I'd rarely felt, and even when I'd felt it, making and keeping friends had never been one of my top priorities. I was thinking this was my opportunity to make a new friend, when I heard footsteps coming our way.

"I wondered where you'd wandered off to." Jake slipped an arm around Stephie.

"Really dude, you can't stay away from her for more than an hour?"

Ace had come over too. It figured.

"We're still newlyweds." Jake gave Stephie a quick kiss.

Ace rolled his eyes. "If you say so."

Jake chuckled. "One day you'll fall under some woman's spell and you'll understand."

"I wouldn't bet on that," Ace said.

Jake smiled at me. "Rumor has it you work with Ace. I'm sorry."

"I've only done one story with him."

"Really? What happened, a cow get out of the fence over at McKinsey's again?"

"I wish," Ace said. "Sadly, it was a cat hoarder."

Jake sighed. "Oh man, that had to be awful."

"It was horrible," I told him. "That poor woman

just kept screaming not to take her babies. I hope she gets some help and support."

Ace stared at me, and anger moved through his body. "*Poor woman*? What about those poor animals? She mistreated and killed almost a hundred cats, and they aren't sure they've even found them all yet. She should go to jail for the rest of her life!"

Rage burned through me. "She's sick. She needs help, not jail."

"She's sick all right."

"Hey, it's a party. Let's all chill." Jake had hold of Ace's arm, and he jerked trying to free himself, but Jake held on. "Why don't we go check on dessert?" Jake pulled, and surprisingly, Ace let him.

"You really have a way with women, Ellison." I heard Jake say. There was what sounded like a growl, and I'm pretty sure it had come from Ace. Good grief! Please tell me he didn't turn into an animal. One shapeshifter in my life was enough.

"Jake will calm him down," Stephie said.

"I can't believe he cares more about animals than people. Animals are great, but they aren't us." It was then that I remembered who I was complaining to. "I'm sorry. I have no business complaining to you about your friend."

Stephie shrugged. "He comes across too strong sometimes. I think he does care about people, he just doesn't want to admit it."

I thought about that for a minute, but it seemed wrong somehow. "I don't understand."

Stephie smiled. "That's because you're such a nurturing person."

My face went hot. "Not really."

"Trust me, I know a nurturer when I see one. Give Ace some time. He's not a bad sort."

"If you say so."

I glanced toward the man in question. Terri was inches from him, talking rapidly and wiggling in that restless way she had. Ace was smiling, obviously enjoying the company.

It figured that those two had connected, but then why wouldn't they? I smiled in spite of myself. Doggie love connection. Those two were a perfect match.

Oddly, I felt a little stab of hurt.

Chapter 4

I arrived at the *Ugly Creek Gazette* the next morning feeling more than a little anxiety. I was thankful for the part-time reporting gig, it helped pay the bills. Still, seeing Ace again wasn't something I looked forward to.

Voices greeted me as I opened the heavy door and walked into the newspaper office. Stephie was standing with Mr. Costa beside the long table. Hope rose in my chest.

"Hi there, Shay. Have you met Stephie Blackwood?"

"Yes, we met last night."

"Good, then you can get right to work. There's a program at Ugly Creek Elementary School in about an hour. They're having a special assembly honoring one of the teachers—only she doesn't know anything about it. You two lovely ladies head over there and get some good stuff for me."

Stephie saluted. "Yes sir, we'll get right on that, sir."

Mr. Costa laughed. "I'm so glad you fell for that Blackwood kid. You definitely belong here in Ugly Creek."

Stephie's cheeks turned pink. "Thank you for accepting me."

Mr. Costa smiled my way. "I predict you'll be next

to become a permanent part of our community."

I shrugged. "Maybe. My aunt certainly loves living here."

"Your aunt is something else," he said. "That woman is full of surprises, but taking off on an around the world tour takes the cake."

"What really surprised us was that my mom and Aunt Rebecca went with her. All three Capps sisters together and taking on the world."

He chuckled as he shook his head. "If the other two are anything like Ruth, the world had better look out."

"If you mean a little…shall we say different, then yes, the world doesn't know what it's in for."

He touched my hand. "It's great having you and your cousin living in Ruth's house while she's gone."

"Thank you. It just seemed to be the best plan for everybody."

"I hate to break this up, but we've got work to do," Stephie said.

My face heated. "I'm sorry, let's go."

"My equipment is already in my car," Stephie motioned toward a little red hatchback. "If you're brave enough to ride with me."

A couple of minutes later we were headed down the road.

"I figured Ace would be the photographer." I smiled. "I gotta admit, I'm glad he isn't. I wasn't looking forward to working with him after yesterday."

"You two do seem to rub each other the wrong way."

"I guess." I looked her way. "I don't mean to irritate him."

Stephie chuckled. "It's easy to get him riled up

over animals. That's actually why he asked me to take work today, he's doing a dog transport."

"A what?"

"Moving dogs from one place to another. Apparently they use some sort of relay system. One person takes the dogs so far, then somebody else takes over." She shrugged.

I considered that for a moment. "So you only work sometimes? I thought you split the photography work."

"Um, sort of. I definitely want to stay in the game, but I spend a lot of time helping Jake at the antique store. Ace takes most of the assignments, and I take over if he needs me, or if I just want to get away from the store, or Jake, for a while."

"Girl, if I was married to the likes of Jake Blackwood, I don't think I'd ever want to take time away."

She laughed. "He's a keeper, but even the best of men can get on a woman's nerves sometimes."

I nodded, "Throw any two people together for a while, and they'll get on each other's nerves."

She glanced at me with narrowed eyes.

"Like your cousin and you?"

"Exactly." And my mom and me, but I didn't want to talk about that. "Aunt Ruth talks a lot about Blackwood Antiques. She loves that place."

"She seems like a very nice person."

I chuckled. "Nice and eccentric."

"I like eccentric." She pulled the car into a parking spot in the front of Ugly Creek Elementary School. "Ready to work?"

"Let's go." I got out and waited while she gathered her cameras. Then we headed inside. This day was

35

certainly turning out better than the last assignment. Honoring a teacher, plus having a nice photographer with me was pretty much a dream assignment.

I tried to ignore an apparently masochistic part of me that missed Ace. I'd have my head examined later. Good grief, between Terri and Ace, some poor therapist was probably gonna get rich. With my money.

I shoved all that aside and got back to playing reporter.

****

The award ceremony with following party was fun, and the teacher seemed to be a really nice, deserving woman. I was still in a good mood when I arrived home. Then I pulled into the driveway and my wonderful day was over.

There they were, both of them, the causes of my upcoming nervous breakdown. Only one was human at the moment, so I spoke to the guy holding the leashes. "Ace? What are you doing here?"

He stomped toward me.

"I brought your dog back. She was at my house. Somehow she managed to get inside my fence and was playing with Hugh."

I glared hard at Trixie, who whimpered softly as she put her head down.

"Don't blame the dog." Ace's voice was rough with anger. "Somebody left her outside alone."

"There's a doggy door—"

"Which should be locked if nobody is home, especially since the fence isn't sufficient to keep her in the yard."

Anger heated my face; this wasn't my fault. "She's Terri's dog."

"Is Terri home?"

I gave the collie another glare before shaking my head. "Apparently not."

The anger in his voice had only increased. "A pet's a commitment. Somebody has to be responsible for them twenty-four-seven."

I met his gaze and held it. "Which is why I don't have one."

"Maybe you should remind your cousin of her responsibility."

"Trust me, I will."

He handed me the rope around Trixie's neck. It was tempting to leave it on her for a while, but I slipped it off and handed it back to Ace. "Thank you for bringing her home."

He nodded, then spun and stomped off down the road. I turned to glare at Trixie, only to find the wayward mutt nowhere to be found. "Please tell me she went into the house." Great, talking to myself. Maybe I should start looking for that therapist. Or a liquor store.

When I pushed open the back door, Terri, naked of course, stood five feet from me, her expression revealing nothing.

"What were you thinking?"

Her bare shoulders moved in half-hearted shrug. "I wanted to play with Hugh."

"You couldn't have just gone as yourself?"

Confusion pulled at her features. "I did."

I wasn't going to beat my head against the wall. I really wasn't. "The human you."

Her confusion deepened. "What fun would that be?"

Fire filled my chest as I took a step toward her so

fast her eyes widened and she leaned away from me. "Do you have any idea what kind of problems you may have caused with your childish little stunt?"

Her mouth hardened into a flat line as her breath sucked in audibly. "Childish?"

My hands tightened into fists. "Yes. Childish."

"Being who I am is not childish."

She wasn't leaning back any longer. In fact, she was right in my face. "I don't have a problem with you being you. I just have a problem with you doing things that could get both of us in trouble. Or at least provoke some very difficult questions."

Narrowed eyes glared at me.

"You're jealous because of my gift."

I blinked. "That's ridiculous."

"You wish you had a superpower too."

Superpower? Who the hell did she think she was? I fought to keep my aggravation in check. "No. I don't."

Terri grinned. "You wish you could write bestselling novels like me. Then you wouldn't have to write silly articles for a tiny newspaper to make money."

Okay, that hit a little close to home. "My articles aren't silly, and I enjoy working at the *Gazette*." At least when Ace wasn't around. "Sure it would be great to be a bestselling author, but I'm not jealous. I'm actually happy for you, and proud to be your cousin."

Her expression relaxed and a little smile pulled at her lips. "Honest?"

"Honest."

She grabbed me in a hug that was sweet, but a little weird, seeing as she was naked and still carried a bit of *parfum de canine*.

When she let go, I smiled. "I love you, silly, even if you are a dog."

"Hack," she said, as she headed toward her bedroom.

"Diva."

"Wannabe."

"Furball."

She firmly closed the door, and I smiled. Terri was a pain in the tokus, but she was the closest thing I had to a sister, and I loved her very much. Even if she was an amazing writer.

Chapter 5

I parked my car in front of Cat Lady's house as my mind swam with reasons to forget this crazy idea and go home. Ignoring my trepidation, I picked up the plastic wrap covered plate of homemade cookies from where it sat on my front passenger seat, then headed toward the porch. The poor woman had been through so much. It'd be great if I could do something to make her feel even a little better.

I knocked on the front door. There was no answer, so I knocked again. "Miz Funderburk, it's Shay Carpenter."

"Go away."

"I have something for you."

"Don't want anything from you."

My eyes stung. "I have cookies. You don't have to talk."

The door opened just enough for me to see an eye and a small slice into the house.

"I don't want anything from you," she said. "Not visit, nor talk, nor cookies. Now go away!"

The door slammed so hard I jumped backward. The smell of cat urine wasn't as strong as the first time, but it was there. As was at least one cat—I'd heard the creature meowing. It had only been a few days and she'd already reverted to her old behaviors. Not surprising really.

I contemplated her situation as I walked to my car. The poor woman didn't want to change. She'd been forced to give up her cats without any kind of support or even kind words. No matter how much her daughter wanted to help her, wanted to protect her, she was fighting a losing battle. I knew from long, hard experience that nothing would work unless Miz Funderburk decided she was ready to get the help she needed.

Back in my car, I tossed the plate of cookies on the passenger seat and headed for home. I'd tried, and that was all I could do. Then again, why I had tried was a big question. It wasn't like I didn't know what the most likely outcome was going to be.

As I pulled into the driveway, I caught a glimpse of Trixie running in the back yard. There was no sign of any other dog, so we seemed to be fine on that front.

I got as far as the porch before I set the cellophane wrapped plate of cookies down and planted my butt on the top step. What the hell did I think I was doing? Hadn't I been through enough with my mom? Was I trying to find somebody else to take care of? The woman had done me a huge favor by telling me to go away.

Out of the corner of my eye, I saw my neighbor poking around the hedge between the properties. Great, an audience. I tried to be nonchalant as I wiped at my eyes. I knew I should go in the house where I didn't have to worry about being observed while crying or beating myself over the head with a figurative ball bat. I didn't though. I loved sitting outside. Our porch back home had been as much a refuge as I ever got. It was where I read, studied, wrote, and worried if my mom was going to kill herself.

I was on the verge of having a major cry fest, when a familiar large gray vehicle pulled to the side of the road near the fence. Out popped Ace, and Miz Carlisle's head came up over the top of the hedge like the periscope on a submarine. Great.

Ace came through the gate, closing it behind him, and headed my way. What now? One of these days I'm gonna learn to hide out somewhere when I'm having a meltdown. Like maybe the top of Mt. Everest.

"Hi, Shay."

Ace sauntered toward me.

"What do you want?" Yeah, I'm a bitch when I'm melting down in public.

I hoped he'd take the hint and skedaddle. Instead he frowned and sat on the edge of the porch near me.

"Are you all right?"

I stared. I flipping stared at this dude who looked exactly like Ace. The guy was a chameleon all right. You never knew what you would get with him. "I'm fine," I lied.

His frown deepened. "I can see something's wrong. If I can help, please tell me how."

I looked into his emerald eyes and saw an amazing thing: concern. Holy freaking crapola. "I just did something stupid, that's all."

"I doubt what you did was stupid."

He was clean-shaven today. His honey-colored hair was sun-streaked. His shoulders were wide and I'd be willing to bet he had a six-pack under that soft green T-shirt.

"Shay?"

I pulled myself out of my daze and looked at him.

Oh yeah, stupid. "Well, it wasn't the smartest thing I've ever done."

He smiled, and I knew I had to derail this discussion before I did something incredibly foolish, like put my hand under his shirt to feel for that six-pack. I picked up the plate beside me. "Cookie?"

He blinked. "Huh?"

"Want one?"

"Sure. Thanks." He pulled up the edge of the plastic wrap and took one of the sugar cookies. He bit into it, his eyes closed and his lips pulled into a satisfied smile. "You made these?"

"Yep."

"You're a good cookie maker."

"Thank you." I couldn't help myself, I watched his mouth as he took another bite. My heart rate kicked into gear, and I felt a little dizzy.

A movement toward the neighbor's yard caught my eye, and I saw Miz Carlisle glaring our way. This was ridiculous. I turned to Ace. "Would you like a glass of ice tea?"

He grinned. "With lots of sugar?"

"Absolutely. Southern boy, huh?"

"Kinda. I was born in Ohio, but I've spent most of my life in Kentucky and Tennessee."

We walked into the house and Ace followed me into the kitchen. "Military brat?" I asked

"Nah, just a mom with a gypsy streak."

He took the glasses from me and set them on the counter while I took the tea pitcher from the fridge. As soon as I poured, he tasted the tea. "You're a Southern girl."

"Yeah, my family's from Tennessee. I grew up in

Jacksonville, Florida."

"Southern Georgia."

"Gee, I've never heard that before."

We laughed as we walked into the living room and sat on the couch. I motioned to where I'd put the plate on the coffee table. "Have all the cookies you want."

He took another one and bit into it. "These really are good."

"Thanks."

My brain registered the click of the doggie door, but I was so caught up in rich forest eyes gazing deeply into mine. It wasn't until I heard movement in the kitchen that it dawned on me what was about to happen. I opened my mouth to suggest we go outside, but it was too late.

"Hello, Ace," Terri said from the open area between the kitchen and living room.

I groaned. As usual after she shifted, she was naked.

Ace's face went blood-red. He got to his feet and stumbled backward toward the door. "I...um...I have to go. Nice to see...oh, hell!" He turned and all but ran out of the house.

I stared at the door, horrified.

Terri laughed. "Now that was funny."

"No, it wasn't." I glared hard at her.

She tipped her head as she studied me.

"You don't even like him."

I sighed, not sure what to say to my clueless cousin.

Her head leaned to the other side. "Socially incorrect?"

"Yes."

"Sorry." She turned and headed off toward her bedroom.

I went to the window and looked toward the road. That Terri had embarrassed Ace shouldn't matter. The man was a pain. I was sure I'd see the humor by morning. I was only worried because I had to work with Ace. I definitely didn't like him. Even if he did have amazing eyes.

Right?

****

When I arrived at the *Ugly Creek Gazette* office the next morning, Ace's big dark gray vehicle sat out front. My face went hot just thinking about seeing him again. Damn Terri. Would she ever understand that dogs and humans had different social norms?

Enough procrastinating. Unlike my cousin, I needed income beyond the royalties from my novels. One deep breath, and I pushed open the door of my car, forced my chin up, and headed toward the inevitable.

When I opened the door both Mr. Costa and Ace turned to look at me. Ace gave a small nod and averted his eyes. Great. The whole day would likely be awkward.

Mr. Costa took a step toward me.

"It's a sad day in Ugly Creek."

"Oh my God, what happened?"

The editor leaned heavily against the nearest desk. "Steve Zapata's computer business was broken into last night. They weren't sure what, if anything, was taken." He shook his head. "Damn, industrial spying. Right here in Ugly Creek. What next?"

"Let's go."

Ace's gentle words shoved me back to reality, and

45

I nodded.

Outside I headed toward my car, only to feel Ace touch my arm.

"There's no use in both of us driving out there, let's take my car."

"Let me get my purse."

I locked my car and climbed into Ace's much bigger vehicle.

He slid into the driver's side. "I know this thing is big, but it's great for transporting dogs."

Well, that *could* explain the big factor. Maybe. "You're really passionate about saving animals."

"Yes, I am. Does that bother you?"

Challenge rang in the voice, as if he was sure I'd say it did.

"No," I told him. "I'm a writer, I understand being passionate about what you do."

His surprise was palpable. "I suppose that makes sense."

We sat quietly for a few minutes before I blurted, "I'm sorry about Terri."

"You aren't responsible for your cousin's actions."

"Still, I should have known that was going to happen. She's totally uninhibited and doesn't always think before she says or does things."

His hand touched my arm.

"Don't do that. Like I said, you aren't responsible for her actions."

"Thank you, Ace. I love my cousin, but she's a little…well…different."

"Aren't writers supposed to be a little odd?"

I leaned my head against the back of the seat. "Yeah, especially when they're *New York Times*'s bestselling authors."

"You're jealous."

Not him too. "No, I'm not."

He grinned. "Yes, you are."

"Okay." I sighed as the irritation slowly dissipated. "I guess I am a little. I can't believe my goofy cousin is doing so well when my advances and print runs keep getting smaller. It's frustrating."

"Maybe it would help if you stopped thinking about Terri and focused on believing in yourself."

I opened my mouth to tell him to go do something physically impossible, but then the truth of his words touched my heart. I swallowed hard. "Maybe you're right."

"Of course I'm right."

Without thinking I smacked his arm, but he just laughed. A moment later, he pulled his car into the parking lot of a four or five story building that wrapped in a half-circle around the back of the parking lot.

The visitor parking area was packed, so he pulled the Xterra into an employee space way back in the lot. "Okay with walking?"

"Sure" Actually I could use the time to get my head out of my rear and into my job.

"Z-Com Tech isn't actually in Ugly Creek, you know. It's a little over a mile outside the city limits."

Interesting. "I take it there's a reason for that?"

"Ugly Creek is unincorporated, and plans to stay that way."

"So they like being a quiet little town."

He looked away and his mouth pulled to one side. "Quiet being the operative word."

Before I could say anything else, we reached the

front. "Z-Com Tech" was written across the big glass doors.

Inside the building, a young receptionist wearing a brown suit and white shirt asked callers to hold while her board flashed so fast it made my head ache just looking at it. When she saw us, she pointed to her right, covered the mouthpiece of her headphone, and said, "Third room on the left."

As we turned away, I saw her stand and slip off her jacket while still answering calls. Poor thing.

A minute later, we entered a boardroom where a harried Steve Zapata talked with a wall of law enforcement, including two men in black suits that screamed federal agent, and a friendlier-looking overweight guy in an Ugly Creek sheriff uniform. Standing near them were two men wearing polo shirts with "Security" written on them. Steve's shoulders were slumped, and there were black circles under his eyes. My heart ached for him.

"Good to see friendly faces." A woman's voice came from behind us.

Ace turned and hugged Liza Zapata. "I feel so bad for you and Steve."

Her eyes had circles too. Her designer suit was wrinkled, and her always-perfect hair was pulled back in a ponytail. She looked at me.

"For the record, some person or persons unknown somehow got past our security last night. We are not sure at the present time what they might have been after, or what, if anything, they took."

I dutifully wrote down her quote word for word. "I imagine you have a great security system."

"State-of-the-art and we don't know yet how the

intruders got through it."

I wrote that down, then closed my notebook. "I'm so sorry. If there's anything I can do, please let me know."

She nodded, glanced at Steve and back to us.

"If you promise to keep it off the record I'll tell you what happened." I saw her swallow. "I need friends right now."

"You know I'm your friend," Ace said

I met her gaze. "I'd never write anything you don't want me to."

We edged farther back from the crowd in the room, and she lowered her voice to a whisper.

"No clue how they got in here, but they did, and stole three million dollars' worth of government contracted equipment and programming."

My breath caught in my chest, and I fought to keep my shock to myself. I shot a glance toward the front of the room. "That's why the FBI guys are here."

She nodded, and her eyes abruptly filled with tears. Before I could move, Ace pulled her into his arms for a long hug.

"I'm here, I'll help you get through this."

I touched her shoulder. "*We're* here."

She looked from one of us to the other.

"Thank you both. It's been rough."

One of the two government agents came toward us and I quickly opened my notebook. "Do you have a statement?" I asked him.

"You're press?"

"Yes." I glanced at Ace. "We're with the *Ugly Creek Gazette*."

He passed a dark look over Ace and Liza, then

turned a less dark but still hard one on me. He'd seen the hug.

"I'm Special Agent Max Killian with the FBI. I can verify there was a break in here last night. The United States' government does have contracts with Z-Com Tech, but so far there is no indication any of that material was tampered with or stolen."

He closed his mouth, and it was obvious from his expression that we had all we would get.

"Thank you," I said. "Let me give you my card. Please call me when you know more." I fumbled in my purse for my newly printed *Ugly Creek Gazette* business cards, but I couldn't find the damn things. I felt my face go hotter the longer I stood there like an unprofessional idiot.

"Here's mine." Ace handed the agent his business card.

The agent nodded, shot another hard look toward Liza, and followed his partner out the door.

"Thank you," I whispered.

"No problem. I'll let you know if he calls."

"I need to talk to Steve." Liza shot a wan smile toward us and headed toward the front.

I was wondering what to do next when I saw the sheriff coming our way. I moved to meet him, opening my notebook as I went. "What is the sheriff's department's plan for dealing with this break in?"

The sheriff shook his head. "This is out of my league, and you can quote me on that, little lady."

"How about we just say your office is investigating, but you don't know anything yet?"

The sheriff, whose nametag read "Richards," smiled as he addressed Ace. "I like her. Madison would have printed exactly what I said, and then made more of it than it really meant."

Ace looked sideways at me. "Madison's a reporter to the core. Shay writes fiction, working for the paper is a part-time job for her."

"You write books?"

My face heated. "Yes, I do. I write contemporary romance."

"So this reporting stuff gets you out of the house."

My stomach churned. I did not like where this was going. "And it helps pay the bills."

He chuckled. "I thought authors were all rich."

There was a twinkle in his eye that had me wondering if he wasn't playing with me. I shrugged. "Only people like Stephen King or James Patterson."

"Yeah, them and that Nora Roberts my wife loves to read."

He looked over my head for a moment, nodding as if contemplating something.

"That Nora does write a fairly good book."

"Yes, she does," I said, fighting the smile pulling at my lips.

He straightened his back as if putting on his official persona. "I'd better get back to work. This is the craziest thing Ugly Creek has ever had to deal with, and that's saying something."

Just what did that mean? "Good luck," I told him.

"Thanks." He turned and strutted off.

"He seems nice." I said.

"He can be."

I looked at Ace, and he shrugged.

"He's the sheriff; he has to answer to all the citizens of our little burg."

"What did he do to you?"

"Later."

I followed Ace's gaze to see Steve walking toward us. The closer he got, the more obvious the circles under his eyes became. My heart ached for the man. What a disaster. The men shook hands.

"Holding up?" Ace asked.

"More or less," Steve said.

I gave him a hug. I figured that was unprofessional and past the boundaries for a person I barely knew, but it seemed like the thing to do. I guess I called it right, because for a moment he seemed to be hanging on to me, as if I was giving him something he needed. Probably he did. Hugs are great relievers of stress. In my opinion, folks don't hug nearly enough.

He let go, and I backed away a step. "Anything I can do for you?"

"Unless you can make this whole mess disappear, I don't think so." His smile was a bit sarcastic with a touch of frustration. He looked up and groaned. "I'd better get back to…" he sighed. "To whatever I have to do next." He went toward a waiting company security guard.

"We might as well go," I said. "I don't think there's anything else we can find out, or do for them."

Ace shook his head. "Unfortunately not."

We headed out to his car. We both sat silently all the way back to the newspaper office. Contemplating, or at least I was, the enormity of the situation. Wow. He stopped at the front of the building.

"See you later, Ace."

He nodded and I headed for my car. I clicked on my seatbelt, put the key in the ignition, and turned it.

Nothing happened.

I checked the gearshift position, made sure everything looked right and my foot was on the brake. I tried again. Still nothing. Crap! I popped the hood and got out to look. I knew the likelihood of me seeing what was wrong was about one in twenty-four hundred million, but what else was I going to do?

"Something wrong?"

I gave Ace a glare. "No, I'm standing here with the hood open because nothing's wrong."

He stuck his head under the hood. "Won't start?"

"Nope."

"I don't see anything wrong."

He checked the tightness of the battery cables and a couple of other things I wouldn't have thought to do. "I can try to boost you off."

"I'd appreciate it." I looked at him, feeling a little guilty about my earlier sarcasm.

He touched my hand, then went toward his vehicle. He pulled in so the cars were nose-to-nose, then hooked the cables to both batteries. When he finished, he looked into my eyes, his expression serious.

"If it starts, go straight to Bryson's Garage."

"Where's that?"

"Turn left at Third, and it's about five blocks on the right. He'll check the battery and alternator for free."

"Thanks."

He just shrugged and headed toward his car.

****

An hour-and-a-half later I pulled into the driveway behind Terri's Fiat. A new battery appeared to have made my car happy, but Ace was right behind me, just to make sure.

I got out and went toward him and he met me halfway. "Thank you so much."

"No problem. I'm just glad it was only your battery." He handed me one of his business cards. "Call me if you need anything."

I reached in my purse and handed him one of my cards.

He gave me a questioning frown.

"I found them when I paid for the battery."

He laughed. "Figures."

We locked gazes and the air between us seemed to shimmer for a moment. He touched my cheek with the tips of his fingers, then turned toward his car. With a quick smile in my direction, he headed toward his house. The man was nicer than I'd thought. Maybe it was because he'd shaved.

"I'd be careful if I were you."

I jumped like a schoolgirl caught daydreaming during geometry class, not that I'd know anything about daydreaming in a math class. "Miz Carlisle! I didn't see you there."

"I tried to warn you before, that Ellison boy is trouble."

The flare in her eyes looked kind of loco to me.

"My car wouldn't start and he helped me out."

Her eyes widened. "I heard on the news about some boys who did things to cars so they could 'help' the girls out."

The woman was beginning to irritate me. "Ace and I were out on a story. We were together the whole time."

She shook her head. "I still don't like it."

"Thanks, but I can take care of myself."

The woman's eyes widened a little too much. "With somebody like him, you never know what he's going to do."

"Um, I really have to go. Thanks for your concern." I backed away a few steps, then turned and walked toward the house, looking over my shoulder every couple of steps.

Once inside, I closed the door and leaned back against it. My neighbor was odder than I thought, or maybe odd wasn't the word.

I realized I was still holding Ace's card. For some crazy reason, feeling it made me smile.

"Our neighbor's nuts, and her cat's the devil's familiar." At least Terri was wearing a robe.

"Devil's familiar, huh?"

She nodded. "That cat loves picking at Trixie. Sometimes Trixie growls at her just for fun."

"You realize how weird what you said sounded, right? And it sounds like the feelings between you and the cat are mutual."

"He started it."

I snorted. Terri glared and stomped into the kitchen. I followed.

By the time I got there, she had her head in the fridge. "What should we have for dinner?"

I shrugged. "We could get a pizza."

"I like the way you think, cousin."

"I need to work on my manuscript anyway." I sighed, the deadline rushed toward me like a brakeless train going downhill.

"I could use some extra word count myself," she said.

"I want lots of veggies."

Terri narrowed her eyes at me.

"I want lots of meat."

"Half with your meat, half with my veggies."

"Sounds good." She got to her feet. "Let me get dressed and I'll go get it. That way I can make sure they make it right."

"Go get 'em."

She stopped just outside her bedroom and looked back at me.

"That Ace dude is cute."

I studied her twitching lips and the mischief flashing in her eyes. "He's nicer than I thought too," I admitted.

"Go get him," she whispered, then turned and disappeared into her bedroom.

I smiled as I sat back and wondered when thinking about Ace had gone from yuck to yummy.

****

A couple of days later, I was in the yard tending to Aunt Ruth's beautiful pink, lavender, and blue azaleas when I heard footsteps on the sidewalk. I looked up to see Ace leading Hugh toward me. He opened the gate on our fence and led the dog into our yard.

"Is Trixie around?" he asked. "Hugh said he wanted to play with her."

I stood and stepped out of the rock perimeter flowerbed. "Said, huh?"

"Dogs have their own way of communicating."

"That's true." I glanced toward my car, the only one in the driveway. "Sorry, but Terri took Trixie to the vet."

"Something wrong?"

"No, just some shots or something."

Ace scratched Hugh's head. "Sorry, boy. Maybe next time."

Did that dog look sad?

"Would you like something to drink?" I glanced back and forth. "Either of you?"

"Thank you, but I think I'd better get this troublemaker back home."

I wasn't disappointed, or if I was, it was because I wanted to see Hugh. Yeah, that was it. Hugh was a very nice dog. I didn't want to see the man. Much.

Ace shifted from foot to foot as he studied the ground. "I do have a favor I'd like to ask."

"I'm good at gardening, writing, cooking, and planning murders."

His gaze shot up, and I grinned.

"You know I do animal transport?" he asked.

"Stephie mentioned that the other day, but I don't know exactly what it is."

"We move animals, usually dogs but it can be anything, from where there aren't homes for them to another where there are. It's a relay. One volunteer takes them so far, then hands them off to someone else who takes them from that spot to another, and so forth."

"Sounds like a great idea."

He nodded. "A lot of animals have found their forever homes because of the animal transport system."

He wasn't telling me something. "So you do this transport thing a lot?"

"Not a lot, really, but I help out when I can." He glanced down, then met my gaze. "I agreed to do a transport this weekend, but I'm in over my head."

Okay, that wasn't what I was expecting. "Over

57

your head? But you do this all the time."

"With dogs." He cleared his throat. "These are cats."

I managed to catch the laugh in my chest before it flew out, although I don't think I got my hand to my mouth fast enough to cover the smile. "Yep. Over your head."

He gave me a dirty look, but then nodded. "Know anything about cats?"

I shrugged. "I had one when I was little."

"Makes you an expert compared to me. Would you like to take a trip tomorrow?"

I resisted the urge to jump on the opportunity like a contract with a huge advance. "Trip?"

"To Nashville to pick up the furry things, then to Atlanta to deliver them, then back here."

I blinked. "That's a long way."

He nodded. "It's actually two legs combined. They couldn't find anyone, so I volunteered. Besides, there might be a couple of Labs that need a ride back here. The coordinator isn't sure yet."

Okay, it wasn't as simple as I'd thought. That was a lot of hours to spend with a guy I wasn't sure if I wanted to kiss or bury in his own backyard.

"I know it's a long way, and you don't know me very well." He took a step toward me.

"And I know you don't trust me."

Damn, he'd taken up mind reading. "Yet you asked me. You must have had a reason."

He shrugged. "I thought maybe it was time we got to know each other. Besides, I really do need the help."

I stared into those warm eyes and realized there was a lot more to this guy than smartass remarks and hair that never stayed in place. I had an opportunity to get to know him, and I really couldn't turn that opportunity down. "Sure, why not?"

He chuckled. "Don't ask that as a question, I might answer it."

Just then, Terri's car pulled in the driveway. Crap! She couldn't have stayed away a few more minutes?

"I think Trixie just got home," Ace said to Hugh. The big dog looked toward the car with interest.

Terri got out, alone of course, and came our way. "Hello, Ace. Hi, Hugh." She reached out to pet the dog.

"Where's Trixie?" Ace asked.

"I told Ace that you'd taken Trixie to the vet."

"Oh," she said. "I did. I, um, I left her at the groomers. I needed to come home to do a couple of things." She smiled as she turned toward the house.

Ace had a frown on his face and I didn't blame him. He turned back to me. "Okay, then. See you tomorrow?"

"When do we leave?"

"I'll pick you up at six."

I was nodding when I realized what he'd just said. "Six? As in *a.m.*? Surely you jest."

He just grinned. "See you in the morning."

Ace and Hugh left, and I followed my cousin into the house. "That was a little too close."

Terri was sprawled on the couch reading a *People* magazine. "Not a big deal."

I jerked the magazine from her hands. "Not a big deal? What the hell would you consider a big deal? Would somebody have to actually see you shift to make it something you'd worry about."

"Chill, Shay. I've handled this my whole life."

She reached for the magazine, which I pulled out of her reach.

"You've always lived in a very rural area. We're too close to our neighbors to be careless."

Terri swung to her feet and jerked the magazine out of my hand, then flopped back down on the couch.

"I'm not careless."

"You don't give much thought to your actions, what would you call that?"

Her gaze locked on mine and her eyes narrowed.

"All I did was go out for a bit. Since when is that a crime?"

I closed my eyes and focused on keeping my temper contained. "You could have let me know you were going out."

The air puffed from her as she let out quick, forceful breaths. "I'm an adult. I don't have to report to you or anybody else."

My jaw was so tight I wasn't sure I could talk. "I'm not talking about reporting to me. I'm talking about letting me know things so that I can cover for you."

She threw the magazine on the couch and stepped right up to me, her nose an inch from mine.

"I'm a big girl, Shay. You don't have to take care of me or cover for me. I'll handle my life by myself, thank you very much."

She spun and marched to her bedroom door, which she slammed behind her. I stood staring at the door, trying to prevent my smoldering anger from flaring into fire. What had Aunt Ruth been thinking when she asked us to move in here together? Would she still have two nieces when she came back from her world tour?

Groaning, I went into my bedroom and grabbed my laptop. Maybe I needed some time to think, and if I managed to get some work done while I was at it, all the better.

Ten minutes later I was at the library. There wasn't a lot of choice in Ugly Creek. God forbid they get a Starbucks. Oh well, it was quiet and I could sulk in peace.

About an hour later, when I had gone from sulk to anger and back to sulk a few times, I'd managed to write a whole fifteen words on my latest manuscript, and I was ready to scream. I knew the deadline was coming up soon, but damn, I just couldn't get into the thing. It wasn't only because of irritation with my immature cousin either. I'd been struggling with the thing for weeks now. I figured it was just the stress of the move from Jacksonville, but even after getting settled in, nothing changed. I hated the characters, the setting, the plot, my editor for offering the contract, and myself for signing it. I dropped my head into my hands.

"You don't have to take the world on your shoulders."

I jumped, but at least I held in the squeal. There was a tiny, vaguely familiar woman standing beside me. Her white hair was up in a simple do. She had wrinkles, but they seemed to fade in the light of her smiling face.

"Excuse me?" I said, for lack of anything better.

She gave a little snort. "You heard me." She held out her hand. "Folks call me Aunt Octavia."

I stood and took her hand in mine. "I've heard a lot about you."

"Interesting things, I'm sure."

That she was eccentric, actually. People also

claimed she was quite the psychic, but I'd ignored that rubbish.

She kept my hand in hers, turning it over so she was studying my palm.

"You have life lessons to learn before you can reach your destiny."

Okay, that didn't compute. "If it's my destiny, what I do doesn't matter."

She shook her head. "Call it your potential, if you like. You are meant to reach that place, but we are always free to choose our own path."

Her finger rubbed my palm as she squinted at something apparently written in the lines and such.

"Let me guess, there's a tall, dark, handsome man in my future."

"Actually, there is."

I rolled my eyes, but she only chuckled.

"But not as a love interest. Your soul mate is part of your destiny, and that's all tied into the life lessons. You won't recognize him until you figure things out." She looked at me with eyes that sparkled with wisdom and mischief.

"Okay, if you say so."

"The spirits say so."

She let go of my hand and stepped back.

"I'll see you in three days. Goodbye, Shay." With that, she walked away.

It was a few minutes before I realized I hadn't told her my name.

"New in town. Family resemblance. Not a hard guess," I muttered. I refused to think about how sure the woman had been.

A thought hit me and I smiled. This Aunt Octavia

was a real character. I could always use a character. She'd definitely end up in one of my books.

With more enthusiasm than I'd had in a while, I went back to my manuscript.

Chapter 6

The deep pounding sounds of the band KISS jarred me from sleep. Groaning, I peeked at the clock. At least she'd let me sleep until four-thirty. As I stumbled to the bathroom, I remembered why it was never a good idea to argue with the likes of my stubborn cousin.

I made coffee, pulled on my clothes, and took a cup out onto the front porch. The temperature was in the fifties, but with my light jacket and hot coffee, it wasn't bad. There, in the deep darkness that is night's attempt to hold back the dawn, I thought about what Aunt Octavia had said about life lessons. It wasn't that I believed her, exactly. It was more an uncomfortable feeling that somehow she had hit on the truth.

Two quick barks caught my attention. The sound was close, but too deep to be Trixie. Then through the soft lamp light coming from the big front window of Miz Carlisle's house, I saw the shadowy shape of a big dog. I groaned. Wherever that canine had come from, it would rile the woman up, and that was the last thing we needed. I'd get a flashlight and a leash and see if I couldn't stop this incident before it got started. Before I could get to my feet, I heard my neighbor's voice.

"What are you doing bringing that nasty creature to my house?"

"I had no other choice," a male voice said.

"You have to get it out of here before dawn," Miz

Carlisle said.

"Fine."

"Don't ever do this again. You understand me?"

Shadowy figures went through the woman's front door, leaving the dog outside and muting whatever answer the male had.

"That's weird," I muttered into the night, then realized what I'd done. "Damn, when did I develop this ridiculous habit of talking to myself?" I grinned. "Oh yeah, at birth."

I sat there, staring into the darkness while my writer's brain threw scenarios at me. What if the man was a foreign agent coming to the house to hide out from the FBI? Why would he go to the home of an old lady? Maybe she was a foreign agent too, or she could be undercover CIA. Nobody would suspect her, that's for sure.

What if I was looking at it all wrong? What if the man was FBI and Miz Carlisle was a contact? He'd come to her to get away from bad guys, or to set up a future sting. Maybe she was a bad old woman, or maybe another FBI agent.

The door opened and the man came out. Through the murky light across the yard, I saw him get the dog and load it into a car, then head down the road away from me. I smiled to myself at my silly theories. Maybe I could write the incident into a book, or use the ideas I'd generated as fodder for a new plot.

I was opening the front door to go back inside when an idea hit me upside the head. This dude could be the tech thief. I had no idea why he'd go to Miz Carlisle, but she seemed to hate everybody, so I guessed she'd be a natural ally. I shook my head as I walked through the living room. That was as crazy as the other theories I'd spun in my head. Right? Maybe I'd mention it to Ace. Except he already disliked my neighbor. Did I want to give him more ammunition?

I sighed and went into the kitchen. Thumping music still came from behind Terri's closed door. What a beginning to the day.

****

Three hours later, I was zooming down Interstate 40 in the passenger seat of Ace's big Xterra thingy. We hadn't said anything to each other except hello when he arrived at my house. I watched the miles rush by and wished I could think of something cute or sarcastic or funny to say. This was boring. And uncomfortable.

Ace must have been thinking along the same lines. "Have you ever been to Nashville?" he asked.

"Yes, actually. I took my mom there once." And I'd vowed to never take her again. She was too anxious to fly, so we drove. I'd taken a week off work and built in fun things to do. I thought she'd love the scenery. I'd chosen Nashville because country music was her favorite thing.

She'd spent the bulk of the drive there sobbing without a sound. On the way, we'd visited Savannah and spent a night at the Chattanooga Choo Choo Hotel, but she could have been a zombie for all the interest she showed. I'd been positive that when we finally arrived in Nashville she'd be at least a little happy to be there. I was wrong. She'd walked through town as if drugged, which was ironic because the doctors couldn't find a drug that helped her.

"Are you okay?"

I jerked out of the pain-inducing ruminations,

embarrassed to have been so caught up in the past. Especially in front of Ace. "I'm sorry, I got lost in my own thoughts. How many times have you been to Nashville?"

"Three, all for dog pickups, although I did manage to do some photography the last time."

"You do mostly animal photography, correct?"

"Yep, actually my work has been published in some prestigious magazines. The newspaper stuff is to supplement that income so that I can do more for the dogs."

"You sure care a lot about those dogs."

He gave me a sideways glance.

"Yes, I do. So?"

There was a sharp, defensive edge in those words. Sheesh. "How many dogs do you have?"

"Three of my own, plus ten rescues that will, hopefully, go to forever homes." The defensive tone of his voice increased.

"Like Hugh."

He nodded. "Like Hugh."

"How do you find homes for them?"

"Getting out as much publicity as we can. Petfinders.com, the Internet in general, local groups, adoption fairs, anything we can do to get the word out."

My ears perked up, and my heart twisted a little. Was he involved with someone? Not that it mattered. Nope, not at all. "We?"

His lips pulled up a little. "Other rescuers."

I was not happy about the lack of mention of a relationship. Nope. Not my business. "That makes sense."

He smiled for real then. "You don't know what to

think about a guy who rescues animals."

"Not the way you do, no."

"It's unusual for a man, true. It's my way of changing the world—at least a little."

"Why dogs? Why not kids, or the environment, or world hunger?"

His lips pressed together and his hands on the wheel got white. "In other words, something that helps humans."

Great, I'd insulted him. "Hey, I love animals. It's just that humans need help too."

"Then you help them."

The sharpness in his tone whipped over me.

I clamped my mouth shut before I said something else that upset him. Damn, he had a trigger a breeze could pull.

Ace reached over and flipped on a jazz CD. I sat back, relieved, and listened to the music. Much better than talking. I let my mind slide away into thoughts of my characters. Not the ones in my current manuscript, other characters who inhabited a story that haunted me. A story that was nothing like what I had always written. A story for which I had no editor or publisher or contract. Characters so very different from my usual fare that I was afraid everyone who read the material would think I'd lost my mind. After all, it ran in the family.

"You like jazz?"

It took me a second to return my mind to the present. "Actually I do. I write to it sometimes, although I prefer silence." I shrugged. "When I do listen, I put on a smooth jazz Internet station, so I haven't put names or titles with anything."

"Maybe I can give you some suggestions."

"I'd appreciate that."

It was quiet again for so long I was beginning to doze off. I know Terri was angry, but why couldn't she find a way to get back at me that didn't involve missed sleep?

"We're early. Would you like to get something to eat?"

My stomach let me know it thought eating would be a good idea. "What did you have in mind?"

"Well, we're meeting the other transporter at Cracker Barrel, so we could eat there."

I shrugged. "Sounds good."

We pulled into the parking lot, and Ace parked toward the back near a grassy area. I was grateful for the short walk. Sitting for hours was not my favorite thing to do—unless, of course, there was a laptop in front of me and I was happily playing in a world that existed only in my head.

Ace's strong hand against my waist gave me no pleasure at all. No tingles. No warm yummies. Really.

We walked into the warm, bustling restaurant. I looked around at the displays of bright, colorful merchandise that was reminiscent of days of long ago and smiled. Since childhood, I'd loved the homey feel and Southern-style food served at Cracker Barrel.

Soon we were ushered into the dining area, and I opened the menu. The photos and descriptions of the food had me realizing how long it had been since breakfast.

"My treat."

I looked at him. "You don't have to do that."

"You're doing me a big favor; let me at least pay

for your lunch."

Mine was a turkey sandwich along with vegetable soup. Ace chose a yummy-looking hamburger with thick meat, and piled high with cheese, lettuce, and tomato. The burger was served with thick, crispy steak fries, and I kept glancing over at his plate, wishing I'd given in to my dark side and risked the calories.

"Would you like a bite?"

I actually jumped. My face went hot as I looked at Ace. "Sorry, I was lost in thought."

The corners of his lips twitched. "Yeah, thinking how much you'd like to have my burger."

My face was on fire. "Of course not, I'm just preoccupied, that's all."

His eyes twinkled as he picked up his knife and cut a nice sized chunk off his burger. He put it on my plate and smiled at me.

"There you go. If you want more, just tell me."

"Ace—"

"Don't even go there. Just eat so we can get out there and meet the cat people."

"Want some turkey sandwich?"

"I'd like that."

I picked up my knife and cut him a big hunk off. I stole some of his fries, and he took a few spoonfuls of my vegetable soup. I began to relax and by the time we got the check, I had decided I was glad he'd asked me on this trip.

Back at his car, we stood on the grass and let the cool breeze blow around us. I was more relaxed than I'd been in a long time.

A blue SUV pulled in next to us and Ace walked toward it as the driver slid out and stood next to Ace.

She was a thirty-something woman wearing a navy track suit and Nikes. She was slim and looked to be in relatively good shape but I somehow doubted she used that suit for much more than errands and transporting animals.

"Barbara?" Ace asked.

"Yes. You must be Ace."

"In the flesh." He motioned toward me.

"This is my friend Shay. She was good enough to keep me company on this trip."

Barbara smiled. "Nice to meet you." She turned back to Ace. "I appreciate you taking on such a long trip."

"No biggie," he said.

They walked toward the back of her SUV and wasted no time moving four small animal carriers from her vehicle to his. In each carrier was a cat, and none of them looked at all happy about the situation.

I went over to the cages and peeked at the furry critters. There was a black and white cat, a tan one that looked to have Siamese heritage, a yellow kitty, and a calico with the biggest blue eyes I'd ever seen on an animal. "They're adorable," I said.

"And that," Ace said, "is the reason I asked her along."

While the two animal people did whatever the hell they did, I talked to the beautiful cats. The calico actually let me pet her with a finger stuck through an opening in the front of the carrier.

"Bonding with the furballs, I see."

I looked up at Ace and smiled. "They're sweet."

"Unlike you." His voice was teasing.

I made a face at him just about the time the tan cat

stuck his paw through an opening in the door and scratched Ace's arm.

"Damn." He looked at me as he backed up. "They don't like me."

"Must be your charming personality."

A little growl came from his throat.

I couldn't help it, I laughed.

"You're asking for it."

His expression was probably meant to be mean, but it looked rather silly to me.

He closed the back while I went around to the passenger seat. For a long time we were both quiet. Somewhere around the halfway mark between Nashville and Atlanta, he said, "What's your favorite color?"

Trick question? Maybe, but there was no obvious good reason not to answer him. "Red."

He grinned. "Figures. I knew you were a hot one."

"Ha ha. What's yours?"

"Blue."

"Figures. Cool and relaxed."

He did that puffed-up-man move. "Yeah, that's me, cool and laid-back."

I rolled my eyes. "You like jazz. Any other music?"

"Lots of different kinds. One Direction, Bruno Mars, some hip hop."

"I lean more toward Adele, Tori Amos, Daya, Kelly Clarkson. And classical."

He raised an eyebrow. "You like Beethoven and stuff?"

"Yes." I gave him a don't-mess-with-me look. "Beethoven is among my favorite composers."

He shrugged. "Whatever doesn't sink your kayak."

The rest of the trip to Atlanta went like that. Teasing banter and information. It wasn't a bad way to travel.

Ace got quiet as we got closer to the metropolitan area, and I knew he was focusing on the traffic. Anybody who's ever driven in, around, or through Atlanta can testify to the crazy lanes, the miles of traffic, and the frequent tie-ups of said traffic.

"You're a good person to do what you do for animals."

"It's the right thing to do."

It was quiet after that, as Ace focused on maneuvering through the rising number of lanes and vehicles. I let my thoughts wander. Music, classical, Beethoven, Tchaikovsky, The Nutcracker, Swan Lake, ballet.

Crap.

My mood dropped like a piano falling out a second-story window. Thoughts danced through my head, a classroom with mirrors on one long wall and barre on the other. The feel of the sweat-soaked leotard and tights, the ache in my legs as I forced them through a difficult step again and again and again. The frustration when the work wasn't paying off, and the sweet feeling of accomplishment when everything fell into place and I felt like I was part of some great cosmic movement

There it was, the smell of sweat and ambition and broken dreams. The realization I could never do the thing I wanted the most.

"Finally," Ace muttered, as he moved into an exit lane and pulled away from the mass of traffic.

Grateful for the distraction, I focused my attention on where we were headed. Before long, he pulled into another Cracker Barrel. "Do animal rescue folks have stock in Cracker Barrel?" I asked.

"It's just a convenient place to transfer." His voice sounded strained, more than just what would be expected from a driver who had just faced the wilds of Atlanta traffic.

Great, now I was going to be riding home with an irritable guy I wasn't crazy about in the first damn place.

He pulled in next to a light blue van with C.R.A.P. written in letters formed from drawings of cats in convoluted positions. In small regular letters below that were the words: Cat Rescue And Protection. "Do they realize their logo is less than professional?"

Ace shrugged. "It gets attention, and that's what it's all about. Attention gets you free publicity, contributions, and interest in adopting."

"I guess."

He ignored me and got out. He went over to meet with the humans, and I headed to the back to talk to the four-legged critters. I was beginning to understand the charm of furry balls that didn't give you crap. Hmm, maybe the group's name had significance after all.

I was smiling at the fuzzy balls of sweetness when a short, square person—no kidding, the woman bore an unfortunate resemblance to Sponge Bob—marched up to me. "Please do not pick at the felines."

"I was just talking to the gorgeous things." I smiled as I touched the paw the sweet faced tan cat had extended through an opening in the door.

"Humph," she snorted, her expression one of a

person who was chronically constipated. She didn't say anything else though.

Another, more normal-shaped, woman joined us, and I backed away from the furballs.

The two women took the carriers to the C.R.A.P. van, and drove away. I went around to the front of our vehicle. I saw Ace, his back turned to me, cell phone to his ear, shoulders forward almost as if he'd just taken a punch in the stomach.

"I'm at the Cracker Barrel," he said. Then, after a pause. "Sure, I'll wait here for you."

I went toward him as he clicked off his phone and turned. "Everything all right?" I asked, though it was obvious something was amiss.

"Damn humans! People don't care about anything but themselves."

My hand touched his arm before my brain kicked in. "What happened?"

"The Labs will be coming with us. The people who adopted them decided they didn't want to fool with two big dogs."

He took a breath, then met my gaze.

"They went through the screening process. They have a large, fenced-in backyard. They seemed the perfect people to adopt two big dogs. Then, after three months, they suddenly decide they don't want to 'fool with them.' Don't they care about the dogs at all?"

"Maybe something happened. Maybe they're getting a divorce, or having a baby, or losing their home, or having to move in a grandmother. There are lots of reasons why they'd need to give up the dogs. Hell, maybe it's breaking their hearts, but they feel they have no choice."

Ace's gaze scorched me.

"Figures you'd defend the selfish humans."

I took two steps toward him. "You're human too, you know."

"Maybe so, but I like animals better than humans."

He moved a little closer, and I did too. "Well, animals are great, but humans are smarter."

"I'm not so sure about that." We were so close I could feel his breath in my face.

The fire in his eyes kicked my heartrate up. My palms itched to flatten myself against his broad chest. "Oh, really." I was all but touching my nose to his.

"Really."

I was gasping. His body almost touching mine had me so distracted I wasn't sure what we were arguing about.

Then his lips captured mine.

Chapter 7

Stop, my brain cried out. Back away from the lunatic! Instead, my rebellious arms slid around his neck, finding muscles I didn't realize he had. My fingers touched him like his skin was Braille, and I was hungry to read his story.

His hands spread over my back and he pulled me close. It felt good to be held. To be warm and secure in the strong arms of a man. Even if they were part of an annoying guy who cared more about dogs than the people around him. That's me, no-life Shay.

I shoved him away. "What the hell do you think you're doing?"

"Me?" His face went red and the muscles in his cheeks and around his eyes tightened. "You're the one who kissed *me*."

"Don't blame me, you're the one who started that kiss."

Ace's shoulders dropped and he closed his eyes for a moment. "We kissed each other."

"Crap." He was right, it had been a mutual touching of lips. My fingers, the same ones that had just caressed Ace's neck and shoulders, touched my still tingling lips as I wondered what had just happened.

"Was it that bad?" His lips were pulled into a crooked little grin.

"Not in the least."

We stepped toward each other. Then I reached for him, and he wrapped his arms around me. This time the kiss was gentle, careful, amazing.

The sound of a vehicle stopping near us registered, but neither of us reacted. The slamming of a car door pulled me out of the experience, and I took a step back. Ace met my gaze with an expression of longing that I knew my face mirrored.

"Ace?"

We turned to see a tall, beautiful woman who shuffled foot to foot as her gaze flicked to Ace then into the distance.

"Yes," Ace said. "You must be Carol."

The woman nodded. "Sorry to interrupt, but I have to pick up my daughter in an hour. I kinda need to get this over with."

"No problem. That's what we're here for."

They moved to the back of her Honda Odyssey and I went to the other side of Ace's SUV to lean against the passenger door. Maybe away from the problem I could get some perspective. I didn't even like Ace. Right?

I glanced over my shoulder. He wasn't bad with that kissing stuff. Oh hell, who was I kidding? His kisses could set a girl's hair on fire.

He was strong too, muscular in a natural way, from hard work, not gym machines. Honestly he was a nice-looking man. Oh great, I was attracted to the annoying obstruction to my highly anticipated new life. Groaning, I leaned my head back and studied the clouds in case some great insight was floating around up there.

I heard the back door of the Xterra opening and looked that way. Ace was loading two large portable cages while nearby, Carol held the leashes of two gorgeous Labs.

I felt myself drawn toward the dogs like Terri is to pizza. "Hello, you beautiful things." I held out my hand to the golden Lab, and then the chocolate brown one. They sniffed my fingers then allowed me to scratch their heads. The golden was about the most beautiful animal I've ever seen, and the chocolate's fur was so soft I wanted to bury my face in it. I have to admit, it wouldn't have been hard to convince me to take the sweet animals home.

It didn't take long for Ace and Carol to get the dogs in the Xterra, and Carol sped off down the road. Ace closed the back of his vehicle, and I made sure I was in my seat before he got in.

The trip to Chattanooga was quiet except for the noise from two big dogs and a jazz CD Ace put in about halfway. There was an awkwardness between us that hadn't been there before, and I didn't have a clue how to deal with it—or him. I slumped in the passenger seat and wished we could go back to the easy banter we'd shared until that damn kiss.

We got to Chattanooga around six and pulled into the parking lot of yet another Cracker Barrel. We both got out and I helped Ace walk the dogs. I was a little nervous about trying to handle such a big animal, but the chocolate was a gentleman and gave me no trouble at all.

We'd been there about twenty minutes when a woman pulled up in a GMC Yukon. At least I was learning a lot about different types of minivans. After all, a writer never knows when she might find herself in dire need of that kind of information.

I kept the dogs company while Ace and the woman did their thing. It wasn't long before they finished and loaded the dogs into the woman's SUV. I got into the passenger seat and didn't look up when Ace got in.

We were back on I-75 and headed home when he said, "There appears to be more between us than a difference in viewpoint."

"Seems that way." I looked at him, and my traitorous body wanted to tell him to pull over so we could do more lip-locking.

He glanced my way.

"That kiss was intense."

"I wouldn't say intense." No way was I admitting that's exactly what it was for me.

"Okay, so we aren't Romeo and Juliet."

Huh? Was he joking? "I hope not."

He laughed then. "Yeah, they didn't exactly come to a good end."

"Not so much, no."

He touched my arm. "I don't want that stupid kiss to mess up our friendship."

"We have a friendship?"

"I'd like to think we do."

"When we aren't arguing."

"I kinda think you enjoy arguing with me."

I opened my mouth to tell him he was nuts, but when I looked his way I realized he was right. I did like arguing with him. Affection warmed my chest and throat, and I smiled at the good-looking pain in my behind. "Busted."

He chuckled as he took my hand in his and squeezed. "We both like jazz."

"Animals."

He narrowed his eyes, then nodded. "Going on drives."

"Thriller novels."

"Roller coasters."

The rest of the drive there wasn't a lot of conversation, but when we did talk, it was friendly and light. Somewhere between Chattanooga and Ugly Creek, I realized there was more to this man than I'd ever imagined. Not sure whether to be happy I knew him or irritated at him for being such a pain that I didn't see his good side until now.

As he pulled in my driveway, I felt an unexpected sadness. "Would you like to come in?"

He gazed over the top of the steering wheel. "I think I'd better get home to the dogs."

I hoped my groan was inward, or at least too quiet for Ace to hear. "I'll make sure Terri doesn't do a repeat of her Lady Godiva entrance."

His smile was weak, and I think the skin of his face shifted in the direction of red.

"Thanks, but I really do need to get home."

I got out, surprised to find Ace coming around the front of his SUV to meet me. He put his hand on my waist, and I felt warm tingles travel up and down my spine."

At the door, he leaned toward me and his lips touched mine. The kiss didn't last long, not nearly long enough in my opinion. Then he turned and got back in his vehicle. I watched as he headed out down the road, giving a brief wave as he went.

"You said you were going to take my advice and stay away from that boy. I hope you don't find out too late that he's trouble."

I moved to confront Miz Carlisle, but she was already marching toward her house. It was probably just as well, I decided. Whatever I said to her would just bounce off her predetermined opinion of Ace.

Sighing, I put my key in the lock and walked into the house. Terri was asleep on the couch, stark naked, her laptop on the floor. I guess it was good that Ace had gone on home. Damn, a girl can't catch a break around here.

I hurried off to the kitchen to round up some dinner. As I threw together a simple casserole, I thought about the day. I'd expected interesting, but not that I might have a great time. Ace was a fun guy to be with, and we had more in common than I'd ever dreamed.

Okay, the pros and cons of getting involved—just physically, mind you. No way was I going to let myself get sucked into some emotional thing. This year was *my* time, getting tangled up with a hot guy was not on my agenda for this year.

Still, Ace interested me in a way no man ever had. Getting involved, even just casually, always carried a risk. But Ace had lip ability that just might make it worth taking a chance.

Chapter 8

Two hours later, I sat at the kitchen table eating chicken and broccoli casserole and typing away at my manuscript. The deadline was approaching, so even if the work was slow, I had to keep going.

"I didn't realize you were home."

"Clearly." I glared at Terri's still naked body.

"Yum, you cooked."

Which was undoubtedly what woke her up. "I'll share if you get dressed."

She made a face at me.

"I can't believe any cousin of mine could be so uptight."

"People usually wear clothes."

"I'm not totally human."

"Boy, isn't that the truth." I shoved a bite of casserole into my mouth while I read what I'd written over the last few minutes.

"Smartass." She headed toward her room.

I rolled my eyes.

"That Miz Carlisle is not a nice woman," Terri said from down the hall.

I didn't look up from the words on the screen. There was something wrong with the last scene, but I wasn't sure what it was. "What's up now?"

"She's always calling me a nasty, stinking animal. She even pokes at me with a broom." The now dressed

Terri scooped casserole onto a plate and sat at the other end of the small table. "Sometimes I growl at that devil cat of hers, just to stir him up."

"She's a character, that's for sure."

"Why do I get the feeling something new happened?"

There was curiosity in my cousin's eyes.

"There was some guy over there this morning, before daylight. She said he shouldn't come there, and he said he didn't have anywhere else to go."

"That's different." She frowned as she shoved in another bite.

"And he had a dog."

Her eyes opened wide. "Dog? At We-Hate-Canines Central?"

"Yep. Any idea what that might be about?"

"Not a clue. But I'll be happy to see what I can find out."

I laughed. "Sleuth Dog to the rescue."

She frowned for a moment, and I was afraid I'd angered her again.

Then she grinned. "Sleuth Dog. I like that."

Terri stood and stretched. "Deadline's calling. I have zombies to kill." She gave me a sideways look. "That doesn't sound right somehow."

I chuckled as she headed toward her room.

She stopped and looked over her shoulder. "I'm sorry about the music this morning."

I put on what I hoped was a stern face. "Just don't do it again. Okay?"

"Okay." She disappeared into her room.

It had been a long day, and I would be perfectly happy to curl up somewhere with a good book. The problem was I had a deadline too, and the damn manuscript wasn't going to write itself. So I got my laptop and sprawled on the couch with it.

By the time I'd booted up the computer a scene was clear in my mind. Unfortunately, it wasn't one from the contracted book, the one with a deadline. Nope, this wasn't a scene from a contemporary romance. This was a dark and haunting story of serial killer stalking a city much like my native Jacksonville. Not a vampire, this man was totally human but lived and killed in ways as gruesome and unnatural as the creatures of legend. I started writing and didn't stop until I was so tired I couldn't continue.

My computer clock said 3:15 a.m., but that couldn't be. I looked at my watch, and the damn thing corroborated the crazy computer. I pulled my stiff body from the couch and checked the microwave and my bedroom clock before I would admit I'd been writing for hours.

Back in the living room, I stood in the middle of the floor and stared at the computer. I hadn't had a writing session that intense for years. What the hell?

I saved and backed up the file and turned off the computer. As I slogged off to bed, I berated myself. Yeah, it had felt awesome flying high like that, but it hadn't put me any closer to fulfilling my contractual obligations. I'd just wasted an entire day, then most of the night. No wonder Terri was a bestseller and I was a midlist author hanging on with local reporting jobs and a few freelance gigs.

I climbed into bed questioning my sanity. First I had kissed Ace, then I'd spent hours writing a side project that would never see the light of day. Were these signs I had inherited my mother's problems? Or even something worse? As I slipped into sleep, I wondered if I'd eventually get too depressed to get out of bed, or maybe voices were going to start whispering in my ear.

There were no voices that night, but I did have steamy dreams of Ace Ellison. At one point I woke sweating and longing for one adorable beach bum. The next dream, though, took a different turn. In this one we were walking hand-in-hand through the woods. Sunshine peeked through the leaves and a gentle breeze blew. The feeling of his strong hand holding mine was exciting and comforting all at the same time. It was magic. Until I woke up.

Dreaming about a guy wasn't irrational, I told myself. Deep down, though, I wondered if I wasn't playing with fire.

****

I woke up the next morning determined to get my head on straight, no matter what that entailed. A stroll through the yard told me the irises and asters needed weeding and the crepe myrtles were starting to fade away. Soon it would get cold and most of them would die out with the first good freeze, but I was going to keep them alive and looking good until then.

Hot, tired, and dirty, I headed for the shower. Thirty minutes later I was clean and full of casserole leftovers. I tried once again to get back to the writing, but I just didn't have any enthusiasm. A walk, I decided, might get my muse stirred up and ready to work. So, I headed out. I didn't know the neighborhood well, so I just walked without knowing where I might end up. I figured wondering around would be a good way to learn about the surroundings.

After twenty or so minutes, I was falling in love with my adopted town. Cute little houses alternated with larger, more elaborate affairs. Green lawns abounded, and it seemed a good portion of the residents spent time outside on those beautiful lawns or on the big porches most houses sported.

I heard barking before I saw where it was coming from. Behind a screen of pine trees, I caught a glimpse of a neatly kept white colonial. I walked a little farther and saw a second building behind the house. Constructed with rectangular blocks, this structure was painted white to match the house. Around the front of the building was shiny silvery fencing that connected with gates to a long enclosed area, and to the main house. I wasn't at all surprised to find the same fencing around the front of the house, or that Hugh greeted me from the other side. He seemed thrilled to show off his friends to me: a scrawny brown mutt, a German shepherd with a bandage on its right front leg, and a scrappy little dog with only one eye.

I rubbed Hugh's head from across the fence, being careful not to scratch my arm on the wires sticking up on the top. "Ace," I called, but even though his SUV was in the driveway, he didn't answer. In the house, maybe?

I pulled out my cell. Ring after ring, but no answer. Was something wrong?

Worry had me pulling open the gate and slipping in before any four-legged critters got away. As soon as I was inside, Hugh, followed by his buddies, headed toward the building behind the house. He looked back at me, and I decided he wanted me to follow.

By the time we got behind the house, I was feeling uncomfortable. It wasn't that I had never poked in places I shouldn't, after all writers are curious people, but Ace was my friend—or something.

"Ace," I called. There was no answer, and my stomach twitched. Maybe something had happened. All sorts of sick, fallen, and torn apart by wild animal scenarios swirled through my active imagination. When I followed Hugh through the partially open door to the long building, what I saw was beyond even my creativity.

Ace sat on the concrete floor in front of several large cages. He held a brown and white dog in his arms. The animal, of a breed I couldn't identify, was so big its head and shoulders were in Ace's lap, but its lower body lay on the concrete floor.

When I caught a glimpse of Ace's face, I came to an abrupt halt. His head was down, and as I watched a tear slid down Ace's cheek, off his chin, and onto the animal. I was beside him before I knew I was moving. "Ace," I said, as I touched his shoulder. "What happened?"

He looked at me as if he hadn't realized I was there.

"Heartworm." He swiped at his face. "The vet and I did all we could, but she just couldn't fight it."

"You must have really loved her."

"She looks like Bear." His voice broke on the last word.

I rubbed his shoulder, hoping my action comforted him a little. "Bear?"

"My brother's dog. I couldn't save her either." His features filled with agony. "Or my brother."

"I'm so sorry." My heart tore, and I wiped at my own tears.

"That was a long time ago." He raked a hand across his face. "Too long for a grown man to be blubbering like an idiot."

I rubbed his shoulder. "There's nothing idiotic about crying, it releases pent up emotion that can cause physical problems—like heart attacks, for instance."

With slow, careful movements, he moved the burden off his legs. He stroked the dog's head before he stood. "There's a clearing out in the woods. I'll bury her there."

"Is there anything I can do?"

He met my gaze.

"Go with me."

I'd been stunned when I found Ace in tears, but that was nothing compared to the emotional hit I took from knowing he was trusting me now. I tried to get the words to come out of my mouth, to tell him I'd be honored to go with him. That his asking me touched my heart. That seeing his reaction had melted a hole through the wall I worked hard to keep between me and other people. I tried to say all that, but the words just wouldn't come. In the end, I simply nodded. It was all I could manage.

He got a sheet and wrapped the dog's body, handed me a shovel, then picked up the animal and the two of us headed out. At the back gate, we slipped through and Hugh tried to follow us.

"Sorry, boy," Ace said. "You can't go, but I'll take you for a walk later, okay?"

Hugh lay down, put his chin on his paws, and gave us a big-eyed sad face. In spite of the situation, I almost smiled at his expression.

It wasn't a long or hard walk out into the woods, but it must have been rough for Ace carrying such a big animal. He showed no signs of fatigue or struggle, though. When we reached the clearing, he gently put down the sheet-wrapped body, took the shovel from me, and began digging like he was trying to dig out the pain in his heart.

"I'd be happy to help you with that," I told him. "I'm pretty good with a shovel."

"I need to do it."

He didn't even look away from his task as he spoke. Hell, maybe he really did need the physical labor to deal with his grief. I'm an only child, so I can't imagine what it would be like to lose a sibling, but if the anguish on Ace's face was any indication, it had to be all but unbearable. I craved more information, but it wasn't the time. Later I'd find out more details, and maybe by then talking would be helpful to him. There wasn't much else I could do.

A movement to the right caught my attention, and I looked that way. What I saw pulled a gasp out of me. "Ace."

He glanced at me, then toward the direction I was staring.

"Hello, Abukcheech." he said.

The creature moved from behind the tree and looked at us with an expression that seemed very human.

"Hello," it said.

I knew my mouth hung open, but I didn't care. The only thing that I cared about at that moment was processing the fact that Bigfoot was standing four feet in front of me. Talking!

Ace stood to face the giant hairy whatever-the-hell-it-was, while I held my breath and hoped the beast was friendly. "This is my friend Shay."

The beast gave me a small nod. "Hello, Shay."

The hair stood up on the back of my neck, but I wasn't about to let Ace be the Bigfoot whisperer. My roommate is a shapeshifter, after all. I took a tiny step toward the creature. "You're for real? I've heard rumors for years, but I wasn't sure something like you was possible."

"We are here," the big critter said.

"Are humans invading your land?" I asked.

The creature leaned his head to one side. "I do not understand."

"Does this land belong to the Dyami?" Ace asked. So, that's what they were called.

The Dyami's face tightened much like a human frown. "Land not belong. Land is."

Like Native Americans. Interesting.

Abukcheech looked at Ace and pointed to the sheet-covered dog. "Animal gone?"

Ace's jaw tightened as he nodded. "I came out here to bury her."

Abukcheech nodded. "I help."

"Thank you." Ace said.

Human and Dyami worked to prepare a grave. Maybe it wasn't as odd as I would have thought that Bigfoot understood burial. No frigging wonder nobody had ever found a body. They must bury their dead.

Ace gently placed the dog into the hole. Tears glistened in his eyes as he took the shovel and refilled the grave.

When Ace finished, Abukcheech went looking for rocks to put over the grave, covering it like a turtle's shell. "Keep animals out," he said.

"Thank you," Ace told him.

The Dyami nodded, then turned and headed back through the trees.

"Wow," I whispered.

"Tell me about it."

He picked up the shovel and together we walked toward his place.

"Why didn't you tell me there were Bigfoot living here?"

"You wouldn't have believed me."

I started to argue, then realized he was right. I'd just seen the damn thing, and I still didn't believe it. Sighing, I wondered what other little surprises lurked in and around Ugly Creek.

When we got back, Hugh was still lying on the other side of the gate, waiting for Ace to return. When he saw us he got up, tail a blur as it wagged.

"Hey, buddy." Ace scratched Hugh's head. "Thanks for keeping an eye on things while we were gone."

The affection Ace and Hugh had for each other brought a smile to my face and warmth to my heart. Hugh seemed to know it had been a rough day for his master, and was going out of his way to cheer him up.

Ace stood to face me.

"Don't look at me that way."

"What way?"

"Like I'm a sad, pathetic loser who cries over losing dogs I barely know."

My jaw dropped. "I don't think that at all. I think

you're a strong, handsome man who just happens to have human emotions like the rest of us."

He gave me a totally unconvinced look.

"Right."

I stepped closer and pressed my palm against his cheek. "No, really."

He touched the back of his fingers against my face. "You're special, you know that?"

My lips twitched in a small smile. "If you say so."

"I do."

Maybe I need my head examined, but he looked so sad, and so cute, that I stood on my tippy-toes so I could put my arms around his neck. I figured he'd shove me away, instead, he put his arms around me and held me against him. He buried his face in my hair and I heard him breathing hard.

He let me hold him longer than I thought he would, then he put his hands on my shoulders and used a gentle but firm push to move me away. He didn't look at me, kept his gaze on the ground.

I stepped back. "If you need anything, or just to talk, you know where I'll be."

His gaze raised briefly to mine. "Thanks, Shay."

When I got to his gate, I looked back. Ace seemed so forlorn I almost turned around. Then I saw that Hugh had taken his place beside Ace, a look on his face that told me he was going to watch out for his master. Feeling better about leaving, I headed back to Aunt Ruth's house. Ace wasn't going to be alone.

Maybe dogs weren't so annoying after all. At least real dogs, not human ones who tended to make their cousin's life miserable.

Chapter 9

I walked into my driveway looking forward to a shower, a quick dinner, and a few thousand words on the manuscript I was contracted to write. I saw Miz Carlisle over by her flowers and smiled her way.

"Shay, can I talk to you for a minute?"

"Sure," I said, going over to the fence. Why can't I just be rude sometimes?

The woman leaned as close to me as the wooden barrier allowed.

"You're going to have to do something about that mutt of yours."

Oh boy. "What did she do?"

"Dug in my magnolias, that's what that huge menace did. It's mean to my sweet Bumpkin too." She gave her baby a smile, and the cat looked up with the most innocent look I've ever seen. Even on Trixie. Dang, that feline was good.

"Well? What are you going to do about it?"

I snapped back to reality. "I'll talk to her."

The woman's eyebrows collided with the steel gray curls on her forehead.

"I mean I'll talk to my cousin. Trixie is Terri's dog."

"I explained the problem to her, but it didn't do any good. Poor Bumpkin is a nervous wreck because of that animal."

I managed a tight smile. "I'll see what I can do."

"You do that." She turned her back and marched toward her house.

Bumpkins looked up at me, and I could swear he smiled. Then he turned, stuck his tail straight up in the air, and followed his owner.

I headed for the house, my mind bouncing between discovering Ace had depths I'd never have imagined and the crazy animal war going on in my own side yard. Well, Aunt Ruth's side yard, the one I'm responsible for until she gets back.

I found my cousin at the kitchen table, munching on a ham sandwich and staring at her laptop screen.

"How was Ace?" she asked.

I groaned. "Let me guess, you smell him on me."

"Actually, I smell dog on you." She sniffed the air once and grinned. "Hugh, for one."

"That is so wrong." I made my own sandwich and plopped down across from her. "Miz Carlisle stopped me outside to complain. Says Trixie dug up her magnolias and is scaring Bumpkin."

Terri rolled her eyes. "That cat could scare Freddy Kruger."

"And the flowers?"

"Why would I do that? If I wanted to dig up flowers, I'd dig up yours."

I was glaring at her when a disturbing thought occurred to me. "It wasn't Hugh, was it?"

Her head jerked up, her expression somewhere between surprise and insult. "He wouldn't go near that loony toon's yard."

I held her gaze. "You're sure?"

"If he were here when I wasn't, I could smell him.

So, yes, I'm sure."

"Maybe it was that dog I saw this morning."

Terri shook her head. "She's been complaining for days. Besides, I barely caught that guy's scent. I don't think he was anywhere near her precious blooms."

I bit into my sandwich, wondering what was digging in our neighbor's yard. "Have you smelled any other animals around here?"

"No," Terri said. "But it could be a gopher or something underground. I wouldn't necessarily have smelled one of them. Then again, I wouldn't put it past the devil cat to dig in the flowers just to cause trouble."

She looked at me with a wide-eyed, puppy expression.

"I'd love to spend hours complaining about Bumpkins the Nightmare Cat, but I have a deadline."

I groaned. "Me too."

We met each other's gazes for an only a writer-with-a-deadline-approaching can understand moment. Then I grabbed the rest of my meal and headed for my bedroom. Like it or not, I had to finish my manuscript.

****

Twenty-four hours and a pathetic, but hard-won, two thousand words later, I stood on the sidewalk of Ugly Creek's historic downtown district. The red-brick building was a classic small Southern town structure, with big windows on either side of the door. A rustic wooden sign hung overhead announcing Blackwood Antiques.

I opened the door and stepped into a spotless store filled with shelves of a mixture of mundane and unusual items spanning at least a couple of hundred years. I was looking around with a case of major curiosity when I caught a flash of robin's egg blue out of the corner of my eye. I smiled toward the wearer of the sweet blouse. "Hello, Stephie. How are things?"

She came around the big counter and moved my way.

Her satisfied little smile suggested her handsome husband had something to do with her mood. "Fantastic. How are you?"

"Fine." I shoved back the little jealous twitch, and smiled. "This store is amazing. My muse is drooling, I think."

She grinned. "I'll be happy to give your muse a friend's discount if there's anything she needs to drool over up close and personal."

I ran a careful finger over a beaded-and-fringed purse that must have been made in the nineteen-twenties. "She might take you up on that."

"Just let me know. Meanwhile would you like a cup of coffee?"

"Sounds good." I walked with her to the back of the store where she poured two cups from a machine behind the counter. "Have you heard anything about the break-in at Steve's business?" I saw the flash of suspicion in her eyes and held up my hands in surrender. "I'm a novelist, not a reporter. I only pull out the journalism degree when fiction doesn't quite pay the bills." I touched her arm. "I saw how Liza and Steve looked after the break-in. I just want to know if they're okay."

Her features softened. "I used to work for a newsmagazine in D.C.; they were serious about sniffing out anything that would sell issues. Not to mention, my best friend is a serious journalist. I learned a long time ago to watch what I said."

"Even with your best friend?" Crap, I'd said it before I thought.

Stephie laughed. "She wouldn't deliberately put me in a bad spot or anything, but if I said something interesting, she'd use what I said as a lead and go chase it down."

She gave my arm a quick squeeze.

"I talked to Liza yesterday, and she sounded terrible. I think she's beyond exhausted. She had to hurry back to work, but she did say things weren't going well."

Emotion filled my throat and I had to swallow before I could speak. "I wish there was something I could do to help them."

"Me too."

The bell over the door tinkled, and a little, older woman dressed entirely in black leather entered the store.

"Aunt Octavia!"

Stephie rushed over to meet her, and I watched as the two embraced.

Octavia's head came up and her gaze snagged mine. Her smile seemed sincere, but there was something about it that twisted my stomach a little.

They walked toward me. "Aunt Octavia, have you met Shay?"

"Of course I have. She's Ruth's niece."

She took my hand in hers and touched my palm gently with the tips of her fingers

"She has an interesting aura, but the spirits aren't telling me why."

I smiled, or tried at least. "Maybe it's my muse

trying to get away from me."

She ignored my attempt at humor by closing her eyes and nodding slightly, as if she was listening to someone only she could hear. When she looked at me again, there was a seriousness in her eyes that caught my attention.

"You have the key," she said.

"The key to what?"

"I don't know. You'll have to figure that out for yourself."

What the hell? "Can't you ask the spirits?"

"The spirits tell us what they want us to know."

"But…"

She put a hand on my shoulder. "Have faith, little sprite."

I opened my mouth to point out that I was taller than her, which was sad since I flirted with five feet, but she was on her way out the door.

"Don't take it personally," Stephie said. "The spirits are always vague."

"You really believe she talks to spirits?"

Stephie's grin took me by surprise.

"Let's just say I learned the strange way that she's the real deal."

I was about to ask her for details, but the door opened and two customers came in together. I sipped my coffee and watched. It was fascinating watching Stephie relating so well with the customers. She was knowledgeable too, throwing out numbers, facts, and historical context like she'd been doing it all her life. I enjoyed watching her so much that I almost forgot that I had responsibilities of my own to attend to.

Unfortunately, my wayward manuscript was due in

less than a month, dang it all, so I snagged Stephie's attention, waved in her direction, and headed back home.

****

I pulled in the driveway to find Terri, Ace, and Hugh standing in the yard. I could see Terri had on her stubborn face. Ace's hands clenched and unclenched at his sides. As I got out of the car, I saw Miz Carlisle pretending to work in her flowers while she watched the show. I thought seriously about getting back in the car and heading out of there. They were adults, after all.

The thing was, I had no idea what Terri would do. Letting something slip would be bad enough with Ace. Miz Carlisle hearing something weird would likely be a disaster. So I headed toward the drama.

Hugh rushed to greet me, stretching the length of the leash in Ace's hand to its max. I scratched his head as I tried to figure out what was wrong now.

"Having a dog is a responsibility," Ace said.

"I take care of Trixie." Terri crossed her arms over her chest.

"Really? Then why does she run around the neighborhood all alone?"

Terri's chin came up. "Trixie can take care of herself."

His face went purple, and I thought Ace was going to have a stroke right there on Aunt Ruth's lawn. "Trixie is an animal. Animals depend on us to protect them. Letting her run loose is not protecting her. It's actually extremely irresponsible."

Terri opened her mouth, but I got between them before she could say something she'd be regretting until her grandpuppies grew up. "Okay, time out!"

"Trixie was at my house again." Ace glared at Terri. "She jumped over the fence and ran away before I could catch her."

Terri glared back at him. "You're just upset because she got away from you."

Well, this wasn't going well. I shot Terri a warning glance. "Can we calm down, please?"

"I don't even know where Trixie went, or if she's all right."

Ace looked worried, and I hated that I couldn't explain. Maybe if it hadn't been for Miz Carlisle, I'd have considered doing just that.

"She's in the house." Terri stuck out her lower lip. "She just wanted to play with Hugh."

"Maybe we can set up play dates," I said.

"Where they'll be supervised." Ace glared at Terri.

"Of course," I said. "Terri, why don't you go let Trixie out so Ace and Hugh can see she's all right?"

Terri stomped off toward the house, and a little of the anxiety tearing at me went away.

Ace let out a long, harsh breath. "That woman is exasperating."

I agreed.

He looked at me, a sheepish expression on his face. "I forgot she's your cousin."

"Which doesn't change the fact that she's exasperating as hell."

He grinned, and my heart rate shot up. What was it about this man that had me so confused? I wasn't sure I even liked him. He was handsome, but not in a Chris Hemsworth sort of way. More like the boy next door. Which, come to think of it, was pretty much what he was.

Trixie ran around the corner of the house and dashed right to Hugh. With what sounded like a groan of defeat, Ace unhooked the leash from Hugh's collar. The two dogs loped off around the yard together. "Okay, she's fine, but you can't blame me for worrying."

"Would you like some iced tea? We could sit on the porch where we can watch the dogs."

"You wouldn't have any of those wonderful cookies, would you?"

He looked so cute I had to smile. "As a matter of fact, I do."

We walked up the front steps, and I left him setting in one of the porch chairs while I went in to get snacks.

In the kitchen I discovered Terri's huge appetite had taken out almost half the cookies. There were enough for Ace and me, though, so I carried the drinks and plate of cookies out, backing through the storm door. Ace met me there, taking the drinks from me and placing them on the table on the porch.

"Thank you."

"No problem."

He gave me a big smile.

We sat. Even though I was aware of Miz Carlisle watching, it still felt comfortable, and somehow right, sitting here with Ace. Until he broke the spell.

"Is Terri coming back out?"

"No, she's in her room, probably sulking."

He grimaced, and I realized why he'd asked.

I touched his hand. "Don't feel guilty about telling her something she should know. She needs to take more responsibility, and not just for her dog."

"Well, I'll tell you then, and you can warn her."

"About what?"

"Mr. Collins's German shepherd disappeared yesterday, and the Martins's Dalmatian vanished a couple of days ago."

"You think somebody took them, don't you?"

"There is no indication they ran away. The families have checked with both local veterinarians, and then they called vets farther away, plus shelters all around the area. I helped them go door to door. No sign of either dog."

"Dognapper?" The word seemed almost cartoonish, except this was serious.

"Yeah, and they should have to watch little Sebastian Martin crying because his dog is gone."

My stomach dropped to my legs, while my heart rose into my throat. "That's horrible."

"It really is. That guy better hope I'm not the one who catches him."

Ace's mouth tightened, and I saw anger in his eyes like I hadn't thought him capable of. All I could think of was that if the dognapper caught Trixie, he'd get the surprise of his life.

"Are you smiling?"

Ack! Busted. "I was just thinking what if the guy got the wrong dog and it took his arm off or something."

"I like that picture, but the likelihood is that he drugs the dogs, probably with a piece of laced meat."

Which Trixie would never eat. Thank God. "Why in the world would anybody want to steal a dog anyway? Aren't shelters full of animals?"

"You have to pay at a shelter, and show I.D."

I didn't want to, but I had to know. "Why would

they want the dogs in the first place?"

"Most common reason is research or breeding. That might be why they took a Dalmatian and a German Shepherd. Thing is, I happen to know they were both neutered."

"Damn, this is Ugly Creek. Things like this aren't supposed to happen here."

He touched his fingers to my cheek.

"I hate to tell you this, babe, but bad things happen everywhere. Even Ugly Creek."

His gaze held mine, and I stopped breathing. The touch of his fingers against my skin felt warm and tingly. He stood so he could put one hand on each of the armrests of my chair, and leaned in. I moved toward him, drawn like a moth toward a wool sweater. Our lips touched and warmth moved through me. This man was more, much more, than I had ever imagined.

Movement to the side caught my peripheral vision. My neighbor was still kneeling in her flowerbed, though she'd stopped even pretending to pull weeds. "Miz Carlisle is watching us," I whispered against his lips.

"Then let's give her something to watch," he whispered back.

His lips captured mine again, claiming me in some primal way. The world around us vanished, and all I felt, touched, or sensed was the connection between me and this amazing man. I slid my arms around his neck, and he pulled me to my feet. Heat blew through me and I tightened my arms in order to get closer to him. His hand slid to my waist and he held me against his hard body. We were on the verge of giving Miz Carlisle the show of her life, when a cat screech and a duo of barking pulled us out of our daze.

He moved slightly faster than I did, but I was right behind him as he raced around the house to where the dogs stood on my side of the fence and Miz Carlisle held Bumpkins on the other. She was making soothing noises to the cat.

Hugh whimpered and pawed at his nose. Trixie alternated between growling toward the other side of the fence and licking Hugh's face. Ace sat on his heels beside Hugh and carefully checked him. From where I stood I could see a long scratch down his snout.

Ace glared toward my neighbor and her feline problem child.

"Your cat hurt my dog."

"If he did, it was because those mean dogs were harassing my sweet kitty. They won't leave him alone. Will they, Bumpkins?" She kissed the cat's head.

"Both dogs are on this side of the fence."

"Bumpkins is on my side."

She glared my way.

"And your furry menace jumps over my fence all the time."

"That's not true," I told her, giving her glare right back. I was aware of Trixie heading toward the house, but ignored that to hold Miz Carlisle's gaze.

She narrowed her eyes. "Like you'd know."

"Excuse me."

"You've had your mind on other things."

She moved the narrow-eyed-glare to Ace, then back to me.

"You can't say I didn't warn you."

"Who I spend time with is none of your business." I hoped my expression conveyed just how insulted I was.

She sniffed. "I told you, I'm a friend of your aunt. I feel I should look out for you."

"Ruth likes me," Ace said, his expression implying that might not be true of Miz Carlisle.

The sound of someone running toward us caught my attention. I looked over my shoulder to see Terri coming up beside Hugh.

She dropped to her heels and stroked his head. Then she stood and crossed her arms over her chest as she glared at Miz Carlisle. "Your cat hurt Hugh."

"As I was telling your cousin, Bumpkins is on my side of the fence. That dog must have jumped over."

"You're lying." Terri's voice was soft, but there was an edge to it.

Miz Carlisle stepped back. "How dare you!"

"I was in the kitchen. I saw your cat come through the fence and attack Hugh."

"I don't believe you." If glares could shoot fire, Terri would be well-done.

"You can believe it or not, but it's the truth." Her face pulled into a knot, the woman took the cat and stomped off toward her house.

"Oh boy." I sighed. "Aunt Ruth won't be happy that we've made an enemy of her next-door neighbor."

"Maybe I should have just stayed away from you." Sadness pulled at Ace's face.

I put a hand on his arm. "What are you talking about?"

"Miz Carlisle hates me because I rescue dogs. She calls the sheriff on a regular basis to complain she hears them bark at night."

"I've never heard your dogs. Ever."

"Me either," Terri said. "She's just an old bitch who hates dogs on general principle. She's always being hateful to Trixie. And that cat is Satan's head demon."

I tried not to, but I laughed a little anyway. "How about we go in the house, where it's more private?"

"I should get Hugh home so I can take care of that wound. Cat scratches can be bad."

"I have first aid stuff."

He smiled. "I'd better go and check on all the dogs."

"I'll see you, Ace," Terri waved and headed toward the house.

He took my hands, and his gaze locked on mine. "Would you join me for dinner tomorrow night?"

Little tingles spread through me. "I'd like that."

"There's not a lot of choice around here, but there's a new place on the far side of town."

"Sounds good."

"See you then."

He kissed me gently.

I watched as he clipped Hugh's leash on him, then headed down the road. How could I have been so wrong about a man?

As I turned, I saw Miz Carlisle peeking around the curtains on her front window. Just for fun I smiled and waved, then headed toward the house.

Chapter 10

I was working on my manuscript—the contracted one—and it was actually going well for once when barking shoved me right out of my fictional world. It would be a major understatement to say I was not amused. A glance at my watch told me it was after midnight, which did nothing to lighten my anger. I was *so* going to kill somebody.

Terri joined me as we headed toward the front door.

"What the hell is going on?"

"No clue, but I intend to find out."

Outside, Miz Carlisle stood on her side of the fence, arms crossed. I could see the scowl from our porch.

"This is what I was talking about. He's probably got those mangy mutts all stirred up to keep good, decent folks from sleeping."

"So you think it's Ace?" As if I didn't know.

"Of course it's that Ellison kid." She let out a loud huff. "Never liked him. There's something wrong with somebody that has that many animals. Up to no good, I'd say."

"Distract her," I whispered.

Terri went down the steps toward our neighbor. I grabbed my cell phone and came back out on the porch.

"Yeah?" Ace's groggy voice said.

"Are your dogs barking?"

"What?"

"Just go open your back door for me, please."

"Sure."

I heard footsteps, then a door opening. There were a couple of quick barks, then silence.

"Okay, now what?"

"Do you hear the barking?" I held out the phone so he could hear better.

"What the hell is going on over there?"

"A frame-up, I'd say."

"What are you...oh hell."

"Yep. Miz Carlisle says that's your dogs."

"Well, you can hear it isn't."

"I didn't think it was, but another witness wouldn't hurt." I walked toward the fence. "Terri, your critique partner wants to talk to you."

She gave me a confused look, then understood. "Hello, Alexandra," she said into the phone. Then turned away.

"The police will be here soon." Miz Carlisle raised her nose in the air and headed toward her house.

Terri handed me back the phone.

"Brilliant," she whispered.

"Still there?"

"Yes, and thank you."

"Just helping out a friend," I said into the phone as I walked back toward the porch. I sat on the step. "She's being vindictive."

"Maybe so, but it's not the first time she's called the cops on me. She did call the cops, right?"

"Yep." I sighed.

"It's a loop," Terri said.

I looked toward where she stood near the steps. "What's a what?"

"The barking is a recording playing in a loop. The same sounds keep repeating." She grinned. "It's like the dogs are saying the same thing over and over."

"She's right," Ace said. "Hear that sharp bark? It'll repeat in a few minutes."

I listened, but before I could sort the sounds out, the barking abruptly stopped. "Interesting."

"Listen closely," Ace said, then I heard him yell, "Squirrel."

Several dogs started barking. I pulled the phone back from my ear, and heard nothing.

"Well," Ace asked. The dogs were already calming down.

"I couldn't hear them. Did you just hear dogs barking, Terri?"

She said, "No," but she nodded slightly and her lips pulled into a smug smile.

So you had to be canine to hear the barking. Maybe Miz Carlisle was a dog. I forced back the laugh. "You're cleared," I told Ace.

"She won't listen, but maybe the cops will." He didn't sound optimistic.

"They're heeeerrrrre," Terri sang.

"Speaking of cops…"

"Call me back when they leave," Ace said, and hung up.

One of the guys from the cat hoarding fiasco got out of the patrol car he'd parked in front of Miz C's house. Terri and I sauntered over to the fence.

"Those damn dogs of Ellison's were barking their fool heads off," she was saying.

"There was barking," I said, "but it wasn't Ace's dogs."

Miz C gave me the evil eye.

"She had her tongue down his throat earlier. Of course she wouldn't believe it was his mutts. It was a bunch of mangy dogs; it had to be him."

"No. It wasn't." I looked at the cop. "I was on the phone with him at the time. His dogs were quiet."

"Like I said, they were making out like teenagers right out in the open in front of God and everybody.

"I talked to him too," Terri said. "His dogs weren't barking."

I could see Miz C's face darken even in the dim light from the moon and the lamp in her window. "They're cousins. They'd lie for each other."

Terri rolled her eyes. "How ridiculous."

"I don't think it's ridiculous," Miz C said.

"Besides," Terri continued undaunted, "the barking was a recording."

"That's crazy!" I wondered if the woman realized she was overreacting, and what that implied.

"It's true." Terri looked at the cop. "It was on a loop, the same sounds repeated over and over."

Miz C. snorted. "Barking is barking. I've never heard any difference."

"Are you sure?" the cop asked.

Terri nodded. "I'm into music, especially classic rock and roll. There are the same types of hills and valleys in music and barking."

"She's crazy." The older woman was red-faced and shaking. I was worried about her.

The cop must have been too. "Calm down, Miz Carlisle. I'll talk to Mr. Ellison."

"Tonight? I have to sleep."

"I have some things to do tonight, I'll talk to him first thing tomorrow."

"If it starts again, I'm calling you."

"Yes, ma'am, you do that."

She turned and marched toward her house.

The cop handed me a card. "If it starts again, give me a call. My cell number is on there."

I nodded, and Terri followed me into the house. "I'm too wired to sleep." I told her. "I guess I'll write some more."

"I might as well start writing now," Terri said. "No use sleeping for an hour or two, then getting up."

"Provided there are no more stunts."

Terri groaned. "That old woman is just plain mean."

I had to agree.

There were no more interruptions, but I never got back into the flow of my story. I went to bed, only to have a hard time going to sleep.

When I finally did manage to drift off, the beautiful erotic dreams I had made it all worthwhile.

****

I woke with serious anticipation of my date with the object of my nighttime adventures. What was with me? Was I even sure I liked this odd guy who could get old women riled up from a mile away? I laughed at the picture that thought provoked, and I gave up the inner debate. Like him or not, he had my body interested in a way I couldn't ignore. Grinning, I headed to the kitchen to make coffee.

I barely got the water in the coffeemaker when a familiar bark had me flying out the backdoor. Trixie growled at a cat's black tail as it disappeared between the boards of the fence and into its own yard.

"Did he hurt you?"

Trixie looked up and shook her head from one side to the other.

I rubbed the soft fur between her ears and looked toward where Devil Bumpkins stood on his front porch meowing piteously. Great. "Let's go inside before—"

"What did that mangy monster do to my baby?"

Miz C trucked over faster than I thought the old biddy could move. She scooped up the little monster.

Too late. "Crap."

Trixie looked at me with an expression of agreement.

I turned to face the accuser. "Trixie didn't do anything."

"It must have done something, because Bumpkins is all upset." She made kissy noises at the cat. "Aren't you, sweetie?"

"I saw your cat go through the fence back into your yard."

"I don't believe you. My little Bumpkins would never go into a yard with a dog in it." She looked into the cat's eyes. "Would you, baby?"

The cat looked up at his owner and meowed softly.

I rolled my eyes. "Come on, Trixie. Let's go in the house."

Trixie followed me through the back door and immediately became Terri.

"That pain in the ass is getting on my last nerve."

"The woman or the cat?"

"Both." She slipped on the bathrobe hanging by the back door.

"So what really happened?"

"Same as always. That devil cat came over here with his fur straight up, his ears back, and hissed and swiped at Trixie. I tried to ignore him, but he kept getting in Trixie's face. She finally barked and he took off through the fence crying like he'd been shot with the water hose. Which I'd like to do, by the way."

"Please don't. As much as I'd like to see that, we have enough problems now." Like my novel, for instance.

Terri sat in one of the kitchen chairs. "So what's up with your writing?"

Oh great, now she was psychic. "What do you mean?"

"Something's been going on for a while now. Every time you sit down at your laptop, you look like somebody stole your cookies."

I looked into eyes filled with true concern and dropped into the chair across the little kitchen table. "It's just something I have to figure out."

She leaned across the table and grabbed my arm. "I know you, and something isn't right. Please tell me what's going on."

"I've written contemporary romance for almost three years, and I've loved it."

"But now?"

"I'm having an awful time trying to finish my contracted book." I studied the flowery tablecloth. "I have this idea for a romantic suspense that just won't let go."

"I could see you writing romantic suspense."

That took me by surprise. "You can?"

She laughed. "Sure. You love *CSI* and *Criminal*

Minds and you read Brenda Novak and Allison Brennan all the time. So how much more do you need for the contracted book?"

"About twenty thousand words."

"Do you have another contemporary contracted?"

"No. Just this one."

"I'll cook breakfast."

She must have seen my expression.

"Okay, I'll get dressed, then I'll cook. While we eat, we can brainstorm ideas to finish your current novel. Then please call your agent and let her know you want to change subgenres."

I groaned. "It's such a big change."

"Chicken."

"Oh all right, the worst she can do is tell me I'm crazy."

"Um, Shay, she already knows that."

I tried to smack her arm but she moved too fast.

I went to get my computer and a notebook for brainstorming. Sometimes having a cousin wasn't a bad thing.

****

I actually wrote two thousand words before it was time to get ready for my date with Ace. That was why I was so excited. Yep, writing was the reason I changed my outfit six times and spent extra time on my makeup. None of that had anything to do with a dog rescuer who irritates my neighbor. Nope.

I looked into the mirror. "Lying to yourself is probably not a good thing."

"Ace is here," Terri yelled.

I rushed to open the door, but Terri beat me there.

"Hello, Ace." Terri's big grin was annoying.

He gave her a quick smile before he looked behind her to meet my gaze. I shoved Terri aside. Ace's smile widened and my heart beat a little faster.

He was dressed in black jeans and an orange shirt that brought out the emerald color of his eyes. "Are you ready?"

"Absolutely," I said. I turned to grab my purse, and Terri gave me a knowing look. I ignored her and went out the door.

As we pulled out of the driveway, I caught a glimpse of Miz Carlisle peeking around her living room curtains. I leaned back in the seat and decided I didn't care; I planned to enjoy the evening. Ace smiled my way, and I knew enjoying would be easy.

The restaurant was beautifully decorated. The entrance and a small lobby-like area were the same shades of red, white, and green as the flag of Italy. Through an arched entryway was a family-friendly area with soft green walls with highlights of red and white. We followed the hostess toward the back and through another arched entryway where we were seated in an adults only area. Here the walls were a richer shade of green, and the lighting was dimmer.

"This is nice, thank you."

He leaned forward and rested his arms on the table. "I owe you an apology."

Huh? "For what?"

"For writing you off as a shallow, spoiled brat."

I let out a quick nervous laugh. "Don't be afraid to open up and tell it like it is."

He took my hand in his. "I reacted to your beauty by believing there couldn't be depth under that adorable face."

Adorable? Was he serious? My face heated. "I don't think I'm shallow."

He grinned. "You're anything but. And you *are* beautiful."

The waiter brought us our drinks, saving me from trying to say something sensible.

When he left, I took a sip of my iced tea before I said, "I underestimated you too, Ace."

"Oh really?" There was that cute grin again.

I nodded. "I thought you only cared about dogs, not people. Now I know you care about both."

He poked his straw against the ice cubes in his tea. "I trust dogs more. Animals don't hurt you the way humans do."

With those words, several things made sense. "Who hurt you, Ace?"

An expression of agony crossed his face, and for a moment I thought he wasn't going to answer. Then he met my gaze. "You know part of it."

"Your brother?"

He nodded. "Mom and Dad weren't the same after he died." He poked at his drink some more. "Dad said they couldn't look at Bear anymore. I begged them to keep the dog, to let me take care of him. But one day I came home from school, and he was gone." His lips tightened as he looked down. "I begged and cried and screamed. I had one major temper tantrum." A sheepish smile pulled at his face. "Normally I'd have been in big trouble, but they must have realized how hard it was for me, so they never said a word about my behavior."

"But you didn't get the dog back?"

"No."

"I'm so sorry."

He shrugged. "It was a long time ago."

"I would have liked to have had a pet," I blurted.

He frowned, but the waiter came with our food before he could ask, so I had a few minutes to wonder what had possessed me to open Shay's Box and let the crap fly out.

As soon as the food was served and the waiter left, Ace caught my gaze.

"Didn't you say you had a cat?"

I poked at my chicken alfredo for a minute while I considered what to tell him. I considered fudging the truth, but he'd been open with me, and he deserved the same. I sipped my tea to moisten my dry throat. "I had the cat when I was little, long before Daddy died. After he got sick, pets weren't really a priority. After he…" I swallowed. "Things were complicated."

He squeezed my hand.

"How old were you when your dad died?"

"Thirteen." My throat filled and I looked down at the table.

"That had to be hard."

"It was, especially when Mom pretty much just gave up." I took a moment to wipe at my eyes and gather my thoughts. "I know depression is an illness, that she couldn't help the way she was, but it was a nightmare." I shook my head, as if the movement would help me let go of the guilt my words provoked. "I know it was hard for her. She suffered a lot."

"So did you."

Tears I'd held inside for years threatened to let loose like a fire hose. I swallowed, determined to keep them in check. "When she finally found a medication combination that worked, I was thrilled. Still am. But I can't help but wonder if—or when—it's going to start all over again."

"Oh honey, I'm so sorry."

It was like being booted out of a dream. I sat up and pulled my hand loose from his. "I'm sorry, I didn't mean to get so emotional."

"Shay."

I looked up as he took both my hands in his.

"Don't do this to yourself," he said.

"This is a date, not my personal pity party." I managed what was probably a pathetic smile.

"Didn't sound like a pity party. To me it sounded more like a woman who doesn't talk about her feelings. That's not healthy, you know."

"Says a man." I smiled for real.

He rolled his eyes. "Eat your dinner before I lecture you about stereotypes."

"It's not a stereotype." I leaned toward him. "You know it's true, men don't like to talk about feelings."

"All right already. You got me."

He squeezed my hands.

"Let's eat. I'm starving."

We spent two hours talking. Just talking. Food, music, movies, how we both hate reality shows, photography, writing, just life in general.

By the time we left, we were laughing together like old friends. When we turned to walk down the sidewalk and Ace put his hand against my waist, I felt safe and cared for. Silly, maybe, but I hadn't experienced a lot of that sort of feeling. So I simply enjoyed it.

We arrived at his SUV, and turned to each other. Our gazes met, and I realized his green eyes were almost black. The way he was looking at me sent heat billowing through my body. He leaned in, pulling me toward him and kissing me with a passion that made my knees weak.

"Maybe we'd better go," he murmured near my ear.

I knew he was right, we were standing on the street. Still, I felt cold when he moved back and opened the door for me. I slid into his car and he got in the driver's seat. He smiled and squeezed my hand, then put his SUV in gear and pulled out of the parking space.

I was surprised when Ace took a side road, but even more so when he pulled into a picnic area at the edge of the woods.

He turned off the engine and looked at me. "I'm not trying to do some teenage parking thing." He grinned. "Unless, of course, you attack me."

"Ha-ha."

"The truth is I just want some time with you without dogs or nosy neighbors."

"Or Terri."

He chuckled. "Or Terri."

The realization that I trusted him was a shock, but a nice one. It felt good to feel safe. And I did with him.

"You realize, that except for going to Zapata's and the transport, we haven't had any time alone together."

He took my hand.

"I'd like a chance to get to know you."

I swallowed. "I guess the guy is supposed to say this, but I'm not interested in a relationship. I've spent my entire adult life taking care of my mom. I'd like to get to know me."

"There isn't any room in my life for a relationship either. You intrigue me though. I'd like to get to know what makes that cute, spunky woman the person she is."

My face heated again, and I did my best to ignore it. "Okay, so we're clear. I will admit you intrigue me too."

"Really?"

"Oh yeah."

He touched his fingertips to my cheek.

"And what is it that you find intriguing about me?"

I looked into those bright eyes that reminded me of sunshine bouncing off a freshly cut lawn. "Your eyes intrigue me," I said.

He chuckled. "What is it about my eyes that interest you?"

"They change shade." I touched his temple near one of those chameleon eyes. "Sometimes they even seem to change colors."

"Do they?"

I nodded. "Green, blue, light brown. The colors are flaked in there, and sometimes the light, or reflection from your clothes, or your mood makes one stronger than the other. At least that's what it seems like to me."

"I love that hair." He wrapped an auburn strand around one finger. "Not only is it a gorgeous color, it's soft and smells like apples."

"My shampoo," I told him.

"It's your personality that really interests me," he said.

"Personality, huh? How's that?"

"You're a little spitfire, but you've been deeply hurt."

He took my hand in his again.

"I got a taste tonight of what that pain is all about,

but I'd love to know more. I want to find out what makes you so skeptical of everybody you meet."

"I'm not skeptical."

He raised his eyebrow at me, and I glared at him. "Just because I was skeptical of you, doesn't mean I am with everybody."

"You still don't completely trust me."

I wanted to deny it, but he was right. "I don't really know you."

"Will you trust me in ten or twenty years?"

My laugh was pathetic. "I'll probably have forgotten all about you by then."

"I'll never forget you," he whispered, as he leaned in to kiss me.

I knew one thing, I'd never forget his kisses. Gentle but strong, he captured my mouth and set the rest of me on fire. I slipped my arms around his neck and held on tight. His tongue found mine, and I wanted the moment to never end.

He slid his hand down my back to my waist while my fingers explored his thick, silky hair. He shifted a little so he was kissing my cheek, my ear, my neck. Oh my goodness, this was incredible.

I opened my eyes for a second as we shifted, and realized we weren't alone. "Ace."

"Sweet," he murmured into my neck.

"Ace, we're being watched."

He raised his head. "Watched?"

I pointed to the furry creature half-hiding behind a tree. I couldn't swear it was the same one I'd seen before, but it was definitely a Bigfoot.

"Abukcheech."

Ace sighed and moved away from me.

"He's curious about humans. He's just a kid, you know."

"Kid?" I looked at the furry critter that was as tall as Ace and half as tall as the tree he was almost hiding behind. "My God, how big are the adults?"

"Nine, ten feet." He put the SUV in gear and backed up.

"Wow."

"Tell me about it. It took a while to take it all in, that's for sure."

Something about the way he said that caught my interest. "What do you mean, all?"

He grinned. "Ugly Creek isn't your average little town."

"Just what else should I be watching out for?"

"You'll find out."

Surprise, and a touch of anger had me narrowing my eyes at him. "You aren't going to tell me?"

He reached over to take my hand in his.

"You wouldn't believe me if I did."

"Ace—"

"Please trust me, honey. It really is better if you find out for yourself. Besides, after three years I doubt *I've* even begun to find out the secrets of Ugly Creek."

I sighed in frustration, but his hand was warm and I had a feeling he was telling me the truth. Good grief, since when did I trust my feelings?

He pulled in my driveway, and kept his hand at my waist as we walked up the steps to the darkened front porch. "I had a great time, Ace."

One hand at my hip and one against my face, he looked into my eyes.

"I'd like to do it again. Soon."

Cheryel Hutton

"Anytime"

He held me gently as he kissed me. I felt feminine, protected, cherished, weird. Not like me to want anybody to take care of me. I was strong, stubborn, a caregiver—not the other way around. So what was going on in my head?

And then I didn't care. All that mattered was that he was holding me and I was holding him.

Finally he pulled away. "I'd better get home."

"Okay." It was all I could think to say.

"Bye, sweetheart."

He turned and walked away, smiling once over his shoulder and giving a little wave as he pulled out.

I smiled back, as relaxed and happy as I'd ever been. I opened the front door.

I was barely in the house when Terri came bouncing out of her bedroom.

"How did it go?"

"Shouldn't you be in bed?"

"Well?"

"It was fun." I knew, even in the dimly lit living room, my smile was giving away more than I would have liked.

Her smile was mischievous. "He must be a good kisser, as long as you two stayed on the porch."

I narrowed my eyes at her. "How do you know we were kissing? Maybe we were just talking."

"Oh, you were kissing."

Something in her expression made me suspicious. "What, did you smell us kissing?"

"No, silly, I heard you."

I groaned. "This is why I don't like dogs."

She kept grinning. "You like dogs."

"No. I do not like dogs."

"You like Trixie."

"That's debatable."

"You like Hugh."

She had me there. "Yeah, I do kinda like that mutt."

"Well, all right then." She did a graceful little twirl to face her bedroom and all but danced through the door.

I headed for bed, and a nice, long, relaxing night.

Of course that couldn't happen.

Chapter 11

Pounding woke me from an interesting dream where Ace and I reenacted the beach scene in *From Here to Eternity*. I pulled on my bathrobe and stumbled into the living room. "Somebody better be on fire," I muttered.

Terri was dressed and answered the door just as I got there. When I saw the uniformed officer, all the clichés flew through my head: toothpick, string bean, Barney Fife. To me, though, he mostly looked like an almost melted snowman, sort of bent forward and looking like his head might fall off his scrawny neck.

"We got a report your dog was outside barking for almost an hour," the melting man said.

"Trixie was in the house all night," Terri told him.

"Are you sure about that?"

"Yes, I am." I saw the irritation in her face. "Plus, I've been awake since three writing."

"What about you," he asked.

"Trixie was inside, and definitely not barking."

"Where is this animal now?"

"She's in the kitchen, I'll go get her." Terri headed that way.

"There have been complaints of barking in this neighborhood several times before," the cop said.

I crossed my arms. "I've only ever heard barking a couple of nights ago."

He gave me a disbelieving cop look. "Dogs never bark?"

"Once in a while, rarely at night." I shrugged.

Trixie trotted into the room and stopped beside me.

There was alarm in the cop's face. "It isn't dangerous, is it?"

Depends on whether Miz Carlisle kept doing this. "No, she's not. Collies tend to be calm and well behaved."

Trixie sat beside me, an innocent expression on her face.

The cop glared at me.

"Don't make me come back here."

"That all depends on whether somebody calls and lies about Trixie again."

He frowned. "So you're saying this was a false report."

Duh! "Yes, sir." I held his gaze until he looked away.

With an expression of mixed irritation and confusion on his face, he headed out the door.

A naked Terri wore an expression that looked like she was ready to bite somebody. "That mean, crazy, vindictive bitch! I ought to go over there and give her a piece of my mind."

"Get dressed first."

"She did this because we saw through her evil plan."

I sighed. "And because I went out with Ace."

"Which is none of her damn business."

"I agree. For some reason she hates him, and because we don't hate him too, she hates us."

"She needs a good kick in the rear."

I nodded. "Unfortunately that wouldn't help anything. We have to be more creative."

A smile pulled at her lips. "If there's something you and I are good at, it's being creative."

"True." I headed toward the kitchen, and coffee, wondering what kind of scheme the two of us could design to sidetrack the resentful old biddy. And her devil cat too.

****

Trixie played in the yard while I sat on the porch with my trusty notebook and pen, trying to get a handle on the next few scenes in my contracted book. Miz Carlisle hadn't come out all morning. Even Bumpkins was indoors. The only sign of life was an occasional tug at a curtain and a glimpse of the side of the woman's face.

A familiar SUV pulled into our driveway, and I felt warmth and lightness fill me. I got to the steps seconds before Ace trotted up them.

"I heard about Trixie getting reported last night. Is everything okay?"

"Other than a burning desire to kick the neighbor's ass, we're fine."

He touched my face.

"I'm sorry. If it weren't for me you wouldn't be tangled up in this mess."

"Oh, Ace." I met his gaze and saw sadness. "It's not a mess, it's just a cranky old woman who doesn't like dogs."

"And her buddies, like Mr. Roark. He reports me almost as much as Miz Carlisle."

"You're kidding? He lives way over on Tremont. No way he could hear Trixie, much less your dogs."

Ace closed his eyes for a moment as he sighed. "Doesn't matter. If they get enough bad feeling going, then I'll be forced to move. Again."

My heart melted. "Come on inside where we can talk."

He glanced toward the door, a worried expression on his face.

"It's safe, I promise."

He didn't look totally reassured, but he followed me inside.

"Trust me," I raised my voice enough to be heard throughout the little house. "There will be no naked cousins, not if she wants to live to finish that bestseller she's writing."

Terri, fully dressed in jeans and T-shirt, came out of her bedroom. "Sorry about before, Ace. At the time, I thought it was funny, but Shay explained to me in no uncertain terms how what I did wasn't socially acceptable." She dipped her chin. "Now that I've had time to think about it, I see her point. I am really sorry, Ace."

"Hey, if anybody knows about social unacceptability, it's me. I spend a lot of time alone with dogs, after all." He held out a hand. "Friends?"

She smiled as she took his hand. "Friends." Then she stepped back. "I'm going to get back to work, I have a book to finish."

"Thank you for backing me up the other night."

"I just spoke the truth." She turned toward her room.

Something she'd said had me wondering. "You aren't almost finished with your book, are you?"

"Yeah, I am. I've got maybe two more chapters."

She looked at me with real concern. "You're still stuck?"

I sighed. "Not stuck exactly, just moving slower than a kid when it's time for chores."

"If I can do anything to help, let me know."

"Thanks, Terri."

She nodded, then disappeared into her bedroom.

I turned to my visitor. "Have you had lunch?"

He groaned. "I knew there was something I was forgetting."

"Come on," I motioned toward the kitchen. "All we have is leftover lasagna, but it's homemade."

"Sounds wonderful."

We'd barely reached the kitchen when my cell phone beeped. It was on the table, so I grabbed it. Maybe I could get rid of the caller and get back to lunch. Then I saw the name. "Hello, Mr. Costa." I heard Ace's barely audible groan.

"There's a fire over on the west side. Can you cover it for me?"

I shot Ace an apologetic glance. "Sure."

"I've got a favor to ask you."

"Okay."

"You live in Ace's neighborhood. Could you go by and see if he can do photos? I've been trying to call him, but he's lost his phone again."

"He's right here, Mr. Costa. Would you like to speak to him?"

"No, just tell him to call me if he can't go. Now get going. The address is 1320 Mockingbird Lane."

"Mockingbird Lane?"

"That's what I said. Now go." He clicked the phone and I looked at Ace. "Fire."

"Oh no. Thankfully my equipment is in the SUV."

As we went out the door I asked, "Is there a 1313 Mockingbird Lane?"

He chuckled. "No. There used to be, but a road cut through there and took out that lot."

"This town is so weird."

We got in and he started his car.

"You have no idea," he said as he backed the SUV up and took off down the road.

"There you go again."

"Sorry." His expression didn't look sorry.

Why did I get the feeling the word boring wasn't in the Ugly Creek vocabulary?

Chapter 12

I saw the smoke long before we arrived at the fire. Apparently, half the town had seen it too, because they were gathered to watch. We had to park a block away and push through a herd of onlookers to get to the house that was on fire.

Volunteer firefighters were already hard at work holding fire hoses that poured water on the house. I didn't see any flames, but smoke billowed out of the doors, windows, and a huge hole in the roof. The air was thick with the smell of wood burning, and my eyes stung.

"I'm going to move around to get some shots."

I nodded. I'd spotted a crying woman standing to one side and holding the hand of a little girl. I headed in that direction. "Are you all right?"

The woman looked at me with huge eyes that were filled with tears. "What?"

"Is there anything I can do for you?"

"She just keeps crying," the little girl said.

I sat on my heels. "My name's Shay. What's yours?"

"Magnolia, but everybody calls me Maggie."

"That's a very pretty name."

"Thank you."

She looked at the house, then back to me.

"When will the fire be out?"

My heart melted. "Soon," I lied.

"Hello, Maggie." A tall woman with the sweetest smile I'd ever seen touched the little girl's head. "How are you?"

Tears filled Maggie's eyes. "I'm scared, Miz Fitz."

"I know, but we'll take care of you. You know Ugly Creek takes care of its own."

A tiny smile pulled at the little girl's mouth. "I know."

Miz Fitz turned to the mother. "Valla."

Valla turned and looked at Miz Fitz with eyes that were large and filled with pain. "It's all gone. Everything is gone."

"I know. I'm so sorry this happened, but we'll take care of you. We'll help you get through this." Then the two women were embracing, and Miz Fitz held Valla while she cried.

I looked at Maggie, and tears ran down her face. "It won't be easy, but it seems like you'll have plenty of support."

Maggie nodded. "Ugly Creek takes care of its own."

That phrase intrigued me, and I considered how to ask about it. And then the world exploded.

My first thought was protecting Maggie, but her mom pulled the little girl into her arms.

Miz Fitz turned to me. "I'll take care of them. Go make sure he's all right."

I shoved through onlookers and firefighters before I realized what she'd said. By then, though, I didn't care. All I could think of was making sure Ace was safe.

Chaos. The entire area was sheer chaos. People

rushed in all different directions. "Propane tank," I heard somebody say. My eyes burned from the smoke, and people seemed to just appear in my way. Frustration tore at me, rapidly morphing into anger. I wanted to scream at the mass of humanity to get the hell out of my way. Then I realized they weren't all human. I can't say what it was that had me thinking that, but somehow I knew.

I shoved my way past a firefighter and saw Ace. He sat on the ground, face and clothes dirty, his camera beside him. He looked up and smiled.

Tears filled my eyes as I flung myself to the ground beside him and threw my arms around him. "You're all right."

"I got one hell of a shot."

I pulled back enough to see his big, excited grin, and smacked him on the arm.

"What was that for?"

"All you care about is a damn picture? You scared me, you idiot. You could have been killed." The tears started again, and I swiped at my eyes.

"You really do care about me."

He grinned again, then wrapped me in his arms and pulled me against him. "Are you okay?"

"I am now."

He kissed the top of my head.

"I'm sorry, honey. I didn't mean to scare you. Trust me, I wasn't trying to get blown up.

"I know." I closed my eyes and took a deep breath, smelling smoke and sweat and male. I didn't want to, but I pulled back, again wiping my eyes. "I need to get some more for the article."

He nodded. "I need some more shots too."

"Don't you dare get hurt, Ellison."

He tipped my chin up.

"You either."

He brushed my lips lightly with his, then we got to our feet and went back to work.

****

Three hours later, we walked into Ace's house. I have to admit, it wasn't what I was expecting. Clean, bright, organized, it was nothing like the messy bachelor pad I'd expected. After all, the guy spent all his time with dogs.

"Let me grab a quick shower and we'll order a pizza or something."

"Pizza's fine." A noise caught my attention and I saw a black metal cage on the other side of the room. Inside was the most adorable dog I've ever seen. I went over and sat on my heels beside the enclosure.

"She's a new rescue, a surrender from a miniature poodle breeder who lives next door to a guy whose prized show dachshund is willing to dig under a fence to see his beloved. Both owners were livid."

The little dog's fur was yellow, a beautiful yellow that looked golden on her. "What's her name?"

"She doesn't have one."

Maybe it was the stress and fatigue, but for whatever reason, tears filled my eyes. "Why not?"

Ace's hand gently gripped my shoulder.

"Nobody wanted her, so nobody named her. You can give her a name if you want to."

"I'd like that," I said, then looked back at the dog, my throat filling with sadness for the little girl nobody wanted.

"You think about it, and I'll go grab that shower."

He headed out of the room.

I opened the cage, and the ball of soft, curly fur hopped out and sat on my lap. She looked up at me with eyes filled with love. I smiled, beginning to see how a person could get attached to something as cute and affectionate as this little thing.

She launched herself out of my lap and sprinted toward the couch, did a skidding turn and ran back at me. I reached to grab her and she ducked my hand to run right past me. She turned again near the front door and looked at me with mischief flashing in her little brown eyes. Then she ran for me again, this time landing in my lap. She climbed up my body, and managed to get close enough to my face to lick my chin.

I laughed and loved the moment before I remembered I hated dogs licking me in the face. But this was no ordinary dog. "Your name is Dusty," I told her as I sat her on the floor.

She gave a little bark to let me know she approved.

A noise caught my attention, and I looked up. Ace stood there, barefoot, jeans, wet hair, and a sunshine yellow golf shirt that brought out his complexion and highlighted the flakes of gold in his eyes. I knew I was staring, but I just couldn't seem to stop myself.

"What do you like on your pizza?"

"Huh?" I realized he'd asked me something, but couldn't for the life of me remember what.

He smiled and pulled me to my feet. "Do I clean up okay?"

"Uh-huh." It was all I could manage to say.

He tugged me against him and covered my lips with his. I melted into his strong arms. Again there was that feeling of being cared for and protected. He slid one hand up and down my back, increasing the feeling of warmth and caring. Slowly a sound drifted into my consciousness, and I looked down at the little ball of fur at our feet.

Ace reached down with one hand and scooped the dog up. "Are you jealous, little one?"

With that, Dusty whined and reached out a paw to touch my arm.

Ace chuckled. "She's already getting attached to you, Shay."

I wanted to be upset. I wanted to resent even the idea of taking on another being to care for. I couldn't, though, not with that little face looking at me. "She's so sweet, aren't you, Dusty?"

"So you did name her, huh?"

I nodded as I scratched her little head. "It fits her."

"That it does."

He looked into my eyes.

"Maybe I should put her back in her enclosure for right now."

He slid his free hand down to my rear, and places in my body I hadn't heard from in a while softened and tingled. "Or we could just order pizza."

"Later," I whispered. "Eat later."

He carefully fastened Dusty in her cage then stood to face me. His fingers trailed down the side of my face.

"You're beautiful." His voice sounded rough.

I couldn't breathe. Ace's warmth and strength pulled at me, and I wanted to lean into him, to give myself into his care. Which made no sense. I was strong. I didn't need anybody. I was the one who was always there for other people. And yet, I needed Ace with my whole being.

I reached my arms around his neck and stood on my tiptoes to touch his mouth with mine. He leaned down to meet me, matching my grasp with his own. One arm held me close, while the other hand moved down and cupped my rear. It was amazing, feeling his touch on me. When that hand moved away, I was ready to grab it and put it back, until he slid it under my shirt. When he touched my breast, I instinctively pressed against it. He kissed me deeper.

I felt his hardness against my belly, and my body caught fire. He released the catch on my bra and slipped his hand under and around until his fingers touched one of my nipples. I gasped, and he repeated the move on the other nipple.

"Ace," I croaked.

He pulled up my top and took one of my nipples in his mouth, licking then sucking. I damn near flew. Then he picked me up and carried me down the hall. He deposited me on an unmade bed, and I registered that the room had a brown sort of feel. I think. And then he pulled my top over my head, and I couldn't possibly have cared less even what planet we were on.

He licked and sucked at my mouth, my neck, my upper chest, and then, dear lord, he took one nipple and then the other in his mouth while his talented hand went south. He touched me in that one place, the one where every nerve a woman has ties into a tiny area where a man can turn her into liquid. He moved away, and I reached for him, but he was busy pulling my pants off me. Okay. That works.

He jerked his shirt off, and quickly shucked his jeans, and then he leaned over me again and I waited in hot anticipation for what he was going to do next.

He kissed me and did some amazing things to my neck and nipples while his hand moved over my stomach and down between my legs. He danced around my magic spot with his fingers until I thought I couldn't possibly take it anymore. I lifted my hips to press my body against his hand, but he wouldn't let me quite reach him.

"Ace, please."

"I want to do this right," he murmured against my neck.

"I can't take much more," I gasped.

"Yes, you can."

He closed his mouth over mine and kissed me like I'd never been kissed before. He took his time getting me right on the edge, then pulling back, licking and tasting my lips, and neck, and belly and lower. He made me forget where I was. Who I was.

He slid my legs apart and moved between them. He pulled a condom on, then leaned over me.

"Ready, sweetheart?"

"Oh, God, yes."

He was gentle as he moved inside me, then took a moment to kiss me. He looked into my eyes and began to move. I watched him as he filled me up, then backed away and did it again. In no time I was ready to go over the edge, but he seemed to know it and stopped.

"You're going to kill me."

He grinned, but I could see the strain in his face.

"You'll thank me."

"When?"

"Now."

With that he began to move hard and fast. Almost

immediately, I lost myself in the midst of a supernova of an orgasm. He followed me right in, and together we experienced the wonders of our own magical galaxy.

A few incredible moments later, he rolled to the side, taking me with him. He brushed my hair out of my face.

"You okay, honey? I didn't hurt you, did I?"

"Are you kidding? That was awesome."

"I was a little worried. You're so tiny."

"Oh good grief, I'm a grown freaking woman."

He grinned. "You're a little spitfire, is what you are."

"So?"

"So, I like spitfires."

He kissed me, and it didn't take long for things to heat up again.

We ordered pizza about midnight, and I called Terri to let her know I hadn't decided to run off to the Bahamas or something, not that I would be opposed to the idea. Then we went back to bed for a lot of lovemaking and a little sleep.

I woke during one of those sleep intervals to see light peeking in the window. I snuggled closer to Ace. It felt amazing to be here with him. It was such a rare experience to let go for a while and not have to be the serious, responsible one.

I was drifting back to sleep when a thought brought me fully awake. I was falling in love with this man. Oh, this wasn't good. I did not need to get myself involved with anybody. I came to Ugly Creek to start over. I wanted freedom, my own life, to get my career going strong. It was bad enough living with an immature, socially backward, shape-shifting cousin. I sure didn't need a man on top of that.

And what happened if Mom relapsed? It was a sure bet a man would want nothing to do with a woman who had to take care of a mother who got so depressed she couldn't function.

I was in deep doo-doo.

Chapter 13

Ace took me home mid-morning. We walked hand-in-hand up the two steps to my porch. "Would you like to come in?"

He shook his head. "I'd better get my errands done and go back home."

"It was great." Well, that was totally inadequate. And I call myself a writer?

He chuckled. "That, my beautiful Shay, was the understatement of the millennia."

His gaze met mine, and electricity flashed between us. Then he held me in his arms, and we kissed. And oh my, the man could kiss.

A buzzing sounded and Ace pulled his cell phone out of his pocket. "Why is it I keep finding this damn thing?" he muttered, then stuck said damn thing to his ear. "Ellison." His expression darkened. "When did you see him last? I'll drive around, see if I can find him." He clicked off the phone.

"Something wrong?"

He nodded. "Mark is one of the high school kids who helps me with the rescues. He just called to tell me his dog, Charlie, is missing."

A chill went through me. "The dognappers?"

Ace closed his eyes for a moment before he looked at me.

"God, I hope not."

"Is there anything I can do?"

"No, sweetheart. I'll drive around and talk to people. Maybe somebody's seen him"

"What kind of dog is he?"

"Collie."

My breath sucked in. "Like Trixie."

He nodded, and my stomach twisted.

"Keep an eye on her," he said.

"I will."

He hugged me close.

"This disgusting piece of dirt has to be stopped."

"Let me know if there's anything I can do."

"Just keep your eyes open and be careful."

He kissed me, then hugged me against him for a moment before he headed down the steps. He slid into his SUV, and with a quick wave he was gone.

My emotions churned as I looked down the road where he'd just been. Dognapper, collie, worry, excitement. Love. Oh, hell no! I turned to go into the house where I belonged. As I did, I saw Miz Carlisle watching me, and I felt the anger in her eyes all the way across the distance between the houses. I smiled and waved, just to keep her off-kilter, then I trucked it into the house before she could put a curse on me or something.

Terri was in the kitchen. "I try not to eavesdrop, but I heard something about the dognapper."

I dropped into the nearest chair. "A collie's missing, and Ace is afraid the napper might have him."

"Well, that is disconcerting." She sat in another chair, worry pulling at her forehead.

"You watch out."

"I will."

She zoned out for a minute, then looked at me.

"I almost forgot, we have guests coming this evening."

"Guests? Well, aren't you the social collie."

"Actually it's Stephie and Liza. Jake is off on an antiques buying trip, and Steve's busy with the investigation and keeping the business going."

"I'm glad she's coming, but I'm surprised Liza isn't busy too."

"She is," Terri said, "but Stephie talked her into taking a night off and relaxing."

"I'm sure she needs it." My heart went out to the couple.

Terri stuck her head in the fridge as she said, "I wasn't sure if you would be here tonight."

"Bite me." I heard her giggle as I headed to my bedroom. I'd showered at Ace's, but I was in serious need of a change of clothes.

I took a sandwich and my laptop out onto the porch and tried to write. I got a few hundred words, but the feeling that Miz Carlisle was watching me wasn't very conducive to concentration. Still, I puttered along. This was my home, and I'd be damned if I'd let the likes of a crotchety old woman force me off my own porch. When I did manage to get my mind focused on my manuscript, I kept thinking of Ace as the hero. Pleasurable, yes. True to the character, not so much.

Eventually I got tired of struggling and took my laptop into the house. Terri typed away in her bedroom, so I left a note and went for a walk.

Aunt Ruth's house was at the end of a cul-de-sac, and the woods began not far beyond. There was a trail back there, so people must go that way. It looked interesting, so I started out.

A few feet in, I figured out that teenagers were the ones using the trail into the woods. Candy wrappers, empty chip bags, and drink cans were scattered randomly on either side. I swallowed, remembering my fellow high school students talking about the fun times they had, and how they were a pain in their parents' rears. I never did any of the wild stuff. I couldn't because I had to take care of Mom.

Except for that one time I went to a movie with a boy I liked. I told Mom where I was going and what I was doing, but when it got dark she got scared and worried. By the time the guy brought me home, the cops were there because she'd been screaming for an hour that I was dead like my dad. She went into the hospital, I stayed with Aunt Ruth for the remainder of the school year, trying hard to not be noticed at Ugly Creek High School. That boy never spoke to me again. I shoved the memory back into the little box in a dusty area of my brain where it couldn't hurt me. Well, not much anyway.

I walked for a long time, enjoying the breeze blowing my hair and the freedom to do whatever the hell I wanted to do. It was so quiet out there, so peaceful. I reached a small cleared area and sat on a tree stump.

I was considering heading toward home when I saw something white between red and silver maple trees on the other side of the clearing. There was movement, and I saw it was a horse.

I stood and slowly moved toward the creature until I could see more of the beautiful white animal. There wasn't a saddle or any indication of a rider. Maybe she had gotten out of her fence. Somebody might be looking for her. I moved a little closer. "Hello, beautiful thing. Where did you come from?" I tried to keep my voice low and soothing.

The horse moved, and I froze. "It's okay. I won't hurt you."

The movement stopped and I took another couple of steps toward her. She, at least I thought it was a she, based on the apparent lack of dangly bits, was snowy white. The piece I could see of her tail was a different color, but I couldn't tell what color that was. In the light through the trees, the tail almost looked lavender, but had to be brown or gray or something. "Who do you belong to?"

The horse moved again, and I gasped. There was a single, long, golden horn on her head. "No. It can't be." I stumbled backwards until I tripped over a rock and landed on my rump. "I've lost my mind. I'm crazy. This can't be real."

This was Ugly Creek, and Aunt Ruth always said it was a special place. So did Ace. But this…

The, I refused to even think that u-word, came toward me.

"Don't be afraid."

Oh hell. Now it's talking to me. Or sending mental messages. Or the voices in my head seem to be a unicorn. Oh no, I had thought the u-word.

"You are chosen."

Oh great. Chosen. Chosen to be nuts?

"Chosen to unravel that which is tangled."

"Could you be a little more specific?"

The unicorn turned and walked deeper into the woods. Damn, her tail really was a gorgeous shade of lavender. I got to my feet and rushed after the creature, but it was gone. Vanished into thin air, or so it seemed.

I waited a few minutes, hoping to see her again. When I was sure she wasn't coming back, I headed toward home. We were having guests tonight, and I needed to get my thoughts straightened out. My plans for this evening didn't include having to prove my sanity.

****

When I got home, Terri was busy in the kitchen.

"Tonight's going to be fun," she said.

Then she turned and looked at me, and her eyes widened. "What happened to you?"

"Do you think I could be, well, I mean with Mom and everything..."

"Spit it out, cuz. What do you think you could be? Not a werecat, I'd have figured that out by now."

"Nuts, okay. Crazy. Loony. Insane."

Her forehead creased, her expression like that of a person who'd just heard the weirdest thing she could think of. "Why in the world would you ask that? Girl, you're the sanest person I know."

"But I saw. No, I couldn't have. I mean there's no way. It's impossible. So maybe I was hallucinating, or something."

She shoved me into one of the kitchen chairs.

"What is it you saw?"

"I couldn't have seen it."

She let out a frustrated sigh. "Well, what is it you couldn't have seen?"

"A unicorn."

She blinked four times, then a huge grin pulled at her face. "A unicorn. How great. Oh man, why don't I ever see the cool stuff? I've never even seen a sasquatch."

"It's not cool. It's nuts. I'll wind up like my mother."

Terri put a hand on my shoulder.

"Sweetie, your mom has depression. It's not like she wears aluminum foil hats or something."

"But…"

"No buts." She pulled a wineglass out of the cabinet and poured an inch or so of wine in it. "Drink."

"Now?"

"Right now. You need to chill."

I looked at the glass, figured she was right, and sipped it. Terri sat a plate of cookies in front of me.

"Eat a cookie so you aren't drinking on an empty stomach. Although you could definitely stand to loosen up."

I ignored her and grabbed a cookie. If the wine didn't make me feel better, chocolate chips should do the trick. She puttered around the kitchen for a few minutes, then sat across from me and picked up her own cookie to nibble.

"You know," she said, "one of the reasons I'm staying in her house is that Aunt Ruth thought I would find acceptance here. She said Ugly Creek is a special place, where all kinds of things happen, so that being different isn't a problem here."

"Even for a half-girl half-furball."

"Ha-ha, but basically, yeah. Odd is accepted by the folks here." She made a face. "Except for that mean old biddy next door."

"*She* doesn't fit in here."

"Boy, that's the truth."

Then it clicked. "That's why you weren't freaked out about the unicorn. You already know about the creatures here."

She shrugged. "I knew about the Bigfoot tribe. Dyami, they call themselves. I know there are other creatures too, but Aunt Ruth wouldn't tell me specifics. She said it was better if I found out myself."

"That's what Ace said too." I sighed. "So God only knows what's out there in the woods."

"Or living next door." She glanced toward Miz Carlisle's house, then shuddered.

I laughed in spite of myself. Then I saw the time and realized what I looked like. "Yikes, I need to shower, again, and get myself ready for guests."

She glanced at the clock on the microwave. "I guess I'd better decide on an outfit."

I shot an apologetic look toward Terri. "I'm sorry. I didn't plan on leaving you alone to get things ready."

She waved a dismissive hand. "I made some cookies, put a lasagna in the oven, and straightened up the few things out of place in the living room. We're not messy, that's for sure."

"We don't have time to be messy." With that, I headed to get myself ready.

****

Two hours later, we sat with Liza and Stephie around the seldom used, even by Aunt Ruth, dining room table. Our bellies were full of Terri's homemade pasta, and the calm was soothing. Of course I had to ruin that. "How's the investigation going?" I asked.

Liza looked at her hands for a moment. "It's not. We can't figure out how somebody could have broken in. The police think it was an inside job, but there is absolutely no evidence to prove it. Besides we have a fantastic group of workers and security, most of whom are from Ugly Creek. "The cleaners check out too, although that's the most likely way the theft happened. We outsource the cleaning crew. But they're checked out thoroughly!"

She dropped her head into her hands, and I felt like a heel for bring up the subject.

"Forget I asked. This is supposed to be a fun evening."

"I'll smack her around later," Terri said.

Liza waved her hand. "No, it's okay. Steve's a wreck worrying about everything, so I try not to get upset around him. I've been holding all this worry and confusion and frustration inside, and I feel like I'm going to lose my mind."

"You know you can talk to me anytime," Stephie said.

"Me too. I know you don't know us well, but we're here for you," Terri said.

"Absolutely," I agreed. "And remember, I'm a novelist, not a reporter. You don't have to worry about me sharing anything you tell me."

Liza smiled. "I trust you."

She gave my hand a squeeze.

"I'm glad for the concern, and I'm glad you gave me the opportunity to let the feelings out." She looked around the table. "I appreciate all of you being so supportive."

"It has to be hard to have somebody steal something so important from you."

Tears filled her eyes. "To be honest, I'm terrified this will be the end of our company. I don't know what we'd do if we had to start over. We'd survive, but Steve has put so much of himself into the business, I'm afraid of what losing it would do to him."

She fought it, but she eventually gave in and cried. The three of us got teary-eyed as we worked at comforting her. After her cry, she went to the bathroom to wash her face. When she returned, her back was straight, she'd reapplied her makeup, and she looked ready to take on a grizzly. I still felt bad about bringing up the theft, but maybe she really had needed to let out her feelings.

"Feel better?" Stephie asked.

"Much." Liza put her fisted hands on the table. "Whoever this creep is, he's not going to take everything away from us."

"Hell no!" Stephie said, holding her wine up.

Terri and I agreed, and we all clinked glasses in commemoration of the moment.

"You know, it's strange," Terri said a few minutes later. "Aunt Ruth always talked about how there was no crime in Ugly Creek, yet, just since we've been here there was a major theft at Z-Com Tech and a dognapper. I hope this isn't a trend. I'd hate for this awesome little town to change."

Liza frowned. "Dognapper?"

"Oh yeah," Stephie said. "I heard about that. One of my customers said her little boy's dog was missing."

"The Martins?" I asked.

"Yeah, how did you know?"

"Ace. He's helping look for the dogs."

Stephie leaned toward me, interest blooming on her face.

"Ace? I thought you didn't like him."

Terri grinned. "She's totally reversed her views."

"Oooh, you must give us details."

I felt my face go hot. "I just realized he wasn't the pain in the rear I thought he was. He's actually a very nice guy."

"*Very* nice, apparently." Terri's grin was big, bright, and annoying.

"We enjoy spending time with each other." My face burned. "We really haven't known each other very long."

"Let's give her a break." Liza grinned, her eyes sparkling with mischief. "In a few more weeks there should be some good stuff we can torture out of her."

"I can't wait." Terri was all but vibrating with anticipation.

Time to change the subject. "Either of you know why Miz Carlisle hates Ace so much?"

"That's right." Liza's face filled with sympathy. "You live next to the old biddy."

"Who's Miz Carlisle?" Stephie asked.

Liza leaned in, as if she were afraid the woman could hear her. "From what I've heard, she and her husband moved here years ago. She was never really friendly, mostly kept to herself. Then one day her husband just disappeared. Nobody knows what happened to him, but after that, she got crabbier and crabbier until she turned into the mean old lady she is today."

"Poor thing probably just misses her husband." Stephie looked so sad.

Was it bad that I wanted to laugh?

"You go right on over there and tell her how sorry you are he's gone." Terri leaned back and crossed her arms.

"That doesn't explain why she hates Ace," I said.

Liza's forehead wrinkled in thought. "I heard she hates dogs, and he has a bunch. Maybe that's her issue."

"She hates dogs all right." Terri's eyes flashed fire. "She and that devil cat of hers harass Trixie all the time."

"Devil cat?" Stephie's eyebrows rose.

"Yep. The damn thing comes over in our yard, keeps on until he gets on Trixie's nerves and she barks at him. Then he hightails it back through the fence to act pitiful for Miz Crabby."

I took over before the mixing of pronouns began. "Then Miz Carlisle gets mad at us. She's not reasonable." My stomach twisted and my pulse raced. "She tried to set Ace up one night. She played a recording of barking dogs, then called the police."

"You're kidding." Stephie looked stunned.

"No, Terri realized she'd looped the recording. It was obvious after she pointed it out."

Liza nodded. "Not being a fan of dogs, she wouldn't have noticed the different sounds."

Stephie shook her head. "Wow. Madison said Ace was a great photographer, and an okay guy. Although, for a while there he was a pain in her ass. She and Mac adopted one of his dogs, or more like it adopted them."

"I'll ask around, see if I can find out anything," Liza said.

"Don't worry about it, Liza, you have too much to worry about now. I'll do the snooping." Stephie grinned. "I'm good at it."

"That you are." Liza stood. "I hate to break this

little get-together up, but I really need to get back to work."

Stephie and Liza said their goodbyes on the porch, and as I turned to go back into the house, I saw Miz Carlisle pretending to work in her flowers. I growled deep in my throat, and Terri gave me a startled look. I laughed in spite of myself. This place was always interesting.

****

Two days later Trixie and Hugh romped in Ace's yard as we sat on his porch, drank Cokes, and watched Dusty romp near our seats.

"So, you borrowed Terri's dog just so you'd have an excuse to come and see me?"

I narrowed my eyes and tried to mentally shoot fire at him. "Arrogant, aren't we?"

"Nah."

I grinned. "Actually, I came to see Dusty."

He put his hand over his heart and leaned back in a wildly exaggerated poise of distress. "You wound me, woman."

I smacked him on the arm. "Don't call me woman."

A gray sedan pulled in Ace's driveway, and I recognized the black-suit, white-shirt-clad man who got out.

Ace headed down the steps to meet him. "Special Agent Killian."

"Mr. Ellison." The men shook hands.

By this time I was standing beside Ace, Dusty in my arms, and my curiosity meter on high.

The agent nodded toward me. "Miz Carpenter."

"Special Agent." I held out my hand to him. No

way was I about to be dismissed without thought just because I happened to be female. He shook my hand, but not very firmly, which lowered my opinion of him.

"I hope you're here to tell us you've figured out who broke into Steve's building," Ace said before I could.

"Actually, Mr. Ellison, I'd like to ask you some questions."

Ace shrugged. "Ask away, but I don't know anything about the break-in. Or Steve's business, for that matter."

"Is there someplace we can speak privately?"

"Sit on the porch," I told them. "I'll go out back and play with the dogs."

I sat on the back porch steps and watched Dusty run around near me. I tossed a tennis ball for her a few times then she climbed up beside me and promptly went to sleep. I stroked her soft head while I watched Hugh and Trixie chase each other around the yard. I gotta admit, even after all these years, it was weird knowing my cousin was a dog. Seriously weird.

I heard a car start up just before Ace came around the corner looking confused and just a bit angry. "That guy is weird."

"If you say so."

"He asked more questions about my rescue operations and my dogs than he did about how I know Steve or much of anything that has anything to do with solving the damn case. Personally, I think he's a fruit loop."

I shrugged. "Maybe he's investigating the dognappings."

Ace snorted. "Yeah, like the FBI cares anything

about animals."

I rubbed his shoulder. "Don't let him get to you."

Bright green eyes looked into mine. "You're right. Besides," he rubbed his knuckles gently over my cheek. "I have better things to think about."

Then I was in his arms, and he kissed me with a passion that should have melted my panties. I closed my eyes and let him hold me, let his tongue tangle with mine, let his hand slide down my back to cup my rear.

The sharp bark startled us both, and we looked toward the culprit. Trixie eyed us innocently, a doggie smile on her mischievous little face.

"Maybe we should go in the house," Ace whispered.

"Sounds good."

I scooped Dusty up, and when Ace's back was turned, I stuck my tongue out at Trixie. Once we were inside, I put Dusty in her crate, and turned to find Ace beside me, his eyes dark and his hands reaching for me. I leaned into the firm body of the man I cared way too much about. He tugged me into his arms and lowered his lips to mine.

His hands moved down my body to rest on my rear. He pulled me against him, and my knees buckled under me, trusting him to hold me up. I slid my arms around his neck and let my fingers explore the silky hair that hung slightly over his collar. I whispered his name, and he tightened his hold on me. He was hard, all of him, and my feminine part went soft at the feeling of that hardness against me. One hand slid up and under my shirt to cover my breast. I gasped in spite of myself, and he chuckled.

"Evil man."

"I'm just getting started."

He pulled my shirt up and used his mouth to tease my nipples right through my bra. Before I knew what was happening, my bra and shirt flew in the general direction of a chair, and he licked and sucked my nipples. When he unzipped my jeans and slid his hand down to my most feminine area, I seriously thought I would faint. Before I could recover from that, he scooped me up.

I gasped. "This is getting to be a habit."

"Do you want me to put you down?"

"Don't you dare."

"All right then."

He headed down the hall, and I leaned against him.

He let me slide down beside his bed, which was neatly made up this time. I pulled his shirt out of his pants and ran my hands up his chest. Meanwhile he was busy relieving me of my jeans and panties. I kicked them aside and together we removed clothing from his body.

For a magical moment, we stood there looking at each other while the air between us tingled with our attraction. He reached for me just as I reached for him, and we tumbled into bed together.

I pulled at Ace, wanting his hard, warm body close to mine. He had other ideas, such as kissing my neck, shoulders, fingers, belly, and the sides of my breasts. I instinctively arched my back as I tried to move my nipples toward his wandering mouth.

The rat laughed. "Want something?"

I'd have smacked him but just then he ran his fingers up the inside of my left thigh, leaving hot tingles where he touched. I moaned his name and grabbed his shoulders in an effort to get him closer.

"Oh baby," he whispered.

His hand moved between my legs while his lips finally moved to my nipples.

I think I levitated.

The sound of a package ripping was enough to put me on the brink of takeoff. "Hurry."

"Trust me." He sounded short of breath. "I am."

Then he edged my legs apart, and I gleefully helped him in his effort. He kissed me with a passion that all but sizzled, then he was inside me and nothing mattered but Ace and our connection.

It didn't take long for us to shoot into space together. Past the moon and planets and into the stars we soared. Then, still together, we drifted back to earth.

Ace rolled, pulling me along with him, so we lay side-by-side.

"You're going to be the death of me, woman."

"Don't call me woman." I have to admit, there wasn't much strength behind the words. I was too relaxed and happy to be upset over such a small thing.

He ran his finger slowly over my collarbone.

"Doing anything tomorrow evening?"

"Not really. Why?"

"I was thinking about driving up to Knoxville to check out that new Italian restaurant I keep hearing about."

I fought hard to hold back my smile. "It's supposed to be good."

"Would you like to go with me?"

"Sounds interesting."

He smiled as he leaned in for another kiss. Things heated up, and we made like astronauts again. And again.

****

The sun was dipping behind the mountains when Trixie and I headed home. As soon as we went in the door, Trixie became Terri.

I braced myself for the teasing; no way she didn't know what had gone on in Ace's house. She surprised me, though.

She let out a long yawn as she headed toward her bedroom. "Shower. Bed."

Grateful not to have to deal with her, I went into the kitchen to grab a sandwich. I sat eating and thinking about the day, about Ace, about our relationship. About possibilities for the future. I have a great imagination, okay? Whether or not any of it was actually possible was irrelevant.

Terri, wearing Garfield and Odie pajamas, trotted into the kitchen and pulled out the makings for her own sandwich. "I thought you were going to bed."

"Too hungry to sleep." She dropped into the chair across the table. "Gotta sleep, though. I want to get some serious word count in the morning."

"I thought you were almost finished."

"I am finished. I'm letting that one set for a few days before I go back over it. While I'm waiting I decided to work on the sequel."

I stared. "Good grief, girl. All you do is write or chase butterflies."

She shrugged. "Same difference."

I laughed. "You might be right about that."

Grinning, she put her plate in the sink and headed off to her bedroom.

"Dedication and self-discipline," I muttered to

myself. That's what it took to be a serious writer, and was something I'd been lacking of late. Groaning, I put my own plate in the sink and went to get my laptop. No way would I let a dog show me up.

If I could get my mind off one solidly built beach bum long enough to work. Damn the man.

I smiled as I booted up my laptop.

Chapter 14

The next evening I wore a sky blue dress with just a bit of frill at the bottom. I paired it with a simple black belt and black heels. I knew I looked cute; still I fiddled with my makeup and hair to the point I made myself more nervous than I already was. What the hell was my problem? I'd been out with Ace before. I'd slept with him. Why was I nervous about going to dinner with him?

The answer was so obvious it should have smacked me in the face. I was nervous because I'd spent quality time with him, because I'd made love with him, because I was falling for the man.

Hard.

I closed my eyes and leaned against the bathroom sink. I knew I was in deep. This was exactly what I hadn't wanted to happen. The absolute last thing I needed was to get tangled up with a man. Men were high maintenance, and right now my life was all about letting go of responsibilities, of learning where my place was in the world.

"He's here," Terri said from the bathroom doorway.

I straightened up, did one last check of hair and makeup, and turned to face the evening. What was there to be afraid of, really?

I walked into the living room, and I knew exactly

what I was afraid of: losing my heart to that handsome man. Too late, a voice inside my head sang gleefully. I smiled in spite of it all and walked across the room.

Ace took my hands in his and kissed me gently.

"You look beautiful."

My face felt like I had leaned too close to a just-opened oven. "Thank you."

He put his hand on my waist as we walked to his SUV. He opened the door for me and held my hand while I climbed up. I was grateful too. I really hadn't thought of how high his seats are, and how short I am. Factor in a skirt and four-inch heels, and I was happy to not look like an idiot.

He went around to get in the driver's side, and I caught a glimpse of Miz Carlisle watching us from behind her six-foot-tall sunflowers. Refusing to give in to the juvenile desire to yell something stupid at her, I smiled at my handsome date, and resolved to forget the crazy woman and enjoy the evening.

Instead of taking the road that would lead directly through town and to the Interstate, Ace headed down a side road, slowing as he neared a house with green siding and ragged lawn. When I saw the dog, I knew why Ace had come this way.

A beautiful German shepherd was chained to a tree. The dog had managed to wrap the chain around and around so that he was caught tightly against the tree. I could hear him whining from the road as he pulled against his restraint. A bowl that likely held water was a good three feet out of the animal's reach.

"Poor thing," I murmured.

I realized the car had stopped when Ace opened the door and headed toward the dog and the tree. My hand instinctively gripped the door handle. Not that I was ready to jump out and join him, or maybe I was. All I knew was my heart hurt for the innocent creature, and Ace just might be saving its life.

A noise to the left caught my attention and I saw Chuck Vanetti run out of the house and toward Ace. Well, run is a bit generous, waddle might be a better word.

"Ace!"

He looked behind him, right at Vanetti, but continued loosening the dog's chain. I held my breath as I watched disaster about to erupt.

Vanetti sputtered obscenities as he grabbed Ace's arm. "You have no right to be on my property!"

Ace easily pulled loose and faced the older man. "I was saving your dog's life."

"You need to leave my dog alone."

"You need to take care of him then." Ace glared hard at the man.

"What I do with my mutt is none of your business."

"Take care of your dog. I've already notified the authorities."

Vanetti laughed. "You go right ahead and call whoever you need to." He stuck his finger in Ace's face. "You come on my property again, and I'll introduce you to my shotgun."

"Take care of your dog, and there won't be a problem." Ace turned and sauntered back to the SUV as if he were taking a stroll.

As we pulled away, Vanetti stuck up his middle finger.

"I had no idea there were people like that in Ugly Creek."

Ace squeezed my hand. "Thankfully, not very many."

"I hope the authorities do something about the situation."

"Me too, but I have my doubts. Animal control services are almost a joke in Ugly Creek. I guess it's because mistreatment of animals is so rare here."

"It's an odd little town." I said.

He let out a short laugh. "That it is."

There was still enough daylight on the drive to Knoxville to see the beautiful autumn colors covering the mountainsides. In fact, the sunset caused the red and yellows and browns and greens to go all fiery and even more beautiful.

Either because it was new and people were curious, or because the food was excellent, the restaurant was packed.

Ace's expression was apologetic. "They don't take reservations. We can go somewhere else if you'd like."

"Here's fine," I told him. "I'm not in a hurry."

We sat squished together with three other people on a bench outside the restaurant door for almost an hour. The time passed quickly, though, while we talked about everything under the sun.

The conversation continued after we were seated at a table toward the back of the restaurant. We laughed, we shared excellent food, we gazed into each other's eyes. If I hadn't been in love with him before, that night would have done it for me.

We were quieter on the drive back, both of us lost in our own thoughts. As we got close to Ugly Creek, Ace took my hand in his.

"Should I take you home?"

"Wherever we go, I would like to spend time with you, if that's all right."

His smile was warm and sexy. "It's more than all right."

"I...um...I would invite you to my house, but..." I don't want you to find out my cousin's a dog. "With Terri and everything, I'm not sure..."

He squeezed my hand. "We can go to my house, if that's okay."

"I'd like that." My cheeks went hot.

He winked, and my face felt like it burst into flames.

Twenty minutes later, we were in his house and stripping each other as we went down the hall. I fell into the bed and he landed on top of me, but made it better by kissing me all over.

He moved off me and I grabbed at him. He didn't go far, just enough to use his talented fingers to get my body into a state of serious need. I tried to return the favor, but he kept grabbing my hands or moving so I couldn't touch him.

I saw his big grin and narrowed my eyes. "Not fair."

"Life isn't fair, sweetheart."

Then he kissed me until I couldn't remember what country I lived in.

A few, incredible minutes later, he slid inside me.

****

I woke up the next morning with warm green eyes looking at me. Before my brain woke up I blurted, "I love waking up next to you." As soon as I said the words, I turned away. "Sorry."

"Don't be."

165

He put his hand on my chin and turned my face so we were eye-to-eye again.

"I love waking up next to you too."

He pulled me close and I rested my head on his chest. I was warm, safe, cared for. It felt good, so why did tears fill my eyes? I quickly wiped at them, hoping Ace didn't see.

"Are you crying?"

"Sorry, just feeling a bit emotional."

"Wanna talk about it?"

"Not really."

"You told me I shouldn't hold in my emotions."

Me and my big mouth. "I'm not. I'm crying."

He tipped my chin up.

"What's wrong, sweetheart?"

The soft caring in his voice was my undoing, and I sobbed against his bare chest. He held me close, his warm breath in my hair, his hand gently stroking my back. I finally got myself together and went to clean up. When I got back into the bedroom, Ace had his jeans on. He took me in his arms.

"Talk to me, baby."

I glanced down at my naked body. I felt more vulnerable without my clothes. "Let me…I can't…not like this."

He nodded, and I went in search of my clothes. Once I was dressed, I sat on his soft brown-and-tan couch. He sat beside me, turned so one knee was on the couch and he faced me from the side.

I swallowed hard three times, took four deep breaths, and ran my palms up and down my thighs a few times. Finally I decided I had to just dive in. "My mom always had a problem with depression, and after

Daddy died she became severely depressed. She spent time in the hospital, and I stayed with one or the other of my aunts until she came home. She tried different drugs, but nothing worked. A lot of the medications had awful side effects too. It was hard watching her go through that." I wiped at my face, and Ace gently massaged my shoulder.

"Both my aunts tried to get her to live with them, but she wouldn't leave the house where she and Daddy had lived. So it was just the two of us living in a tiny house in Jacksonville. Thankfully Daddy left us with enough to pay off the house and life was okay for a while. Mom stayed in bed most of the time, and I had to cook and clean. I had to go to therapy myself to keep from getting depressed from spending so much time with such a depressed person. By the time I was seventeen, the money was gone and I had to work so we could survive. It was hard, but I made it through high school and then college. I got a job working for a small local newspaper. It didn't pay a lot, but they were flexible with my hours. I hated it from day one. I knew I wanted to write fiction, but I was afraid to try.

"Terri was published by then and she encouraged me. She gave me a lot of advice and told me where I could learn more. She lent me books, paid for online classes. She was great. Eventually I wrote a novel manuscript in my spare time, then another. I was terrified to submit them anywhere, but Terri wouldn't shut up until I did."

"She was right."

I nodded. "It took a while, a lot of rejections, and another manuscript, but I got an agent and eight months later I signed a contract for a three-book deal."

"I'm so proud of you for hanging in there and reaching your goal." He squeezed my hand. "A lot of people give up before they reach their dreams."

I shrugged. "It was something to hang on to. Something to take my mind off the sadness I lived with day after day."

"But your mom's better now, right?"

His words pulled me back to the present—and the problem. "Yes, she's much better. She tried a new antidepressant, and that, along with her other meds and therapy, finally got her on solid ground."

"That's great."

"I think the whole family held our breath for a long time. When a year went by and she was still doing well, the sisters decided to go on a world tour to celebrate."

Understanding brightened his face. "Coming to Ugly Creek was a new start for you."

I smiled, and touched my fingers to his face. "It was really nice of Aunt Ruth to suggest that Terri and I stay in her house for the year she's away."

"I, um, have a question."

"Okay." Trepidation pulled at my stomach

"I understand why you came up here. I'm sure you needed to get away and get a taste of a different kind of life."

"Very astute."

"It's none of my business, and probably just plain nosy, but I'm curious. What brought Terri to Ugly Creek?"

Relief soared inside me. "She lives with her mom, she came up here so she wouldn't be alone."

"She lives with her mother?"

I shrugged. "Her mom lives in the country, so she

has plenty of room to…" I caught myself and rethought my words. "So Trixie has lots of room to run and play."

He grinned. "So she's really attached to that dog, huh?"

I snorted in spite of myself. "You have no idea."

"Hey." He took my hands in his. "Let's go do something fun."

"I like that idea. Where should we go?"

"Hmm, maybe for ice cream."

"For breakfast?"

He shrugged. "More like early lunch."

"Oh why not?" I hugged him. "I need to go home and change first."

"I guess we could wait that long."

I smacked his arm, and we were both laughing when his cell phone chirped.

"Time to lose that damn thing again." He looked at it and groaned. "Hello, Mr. Costa."

He listened for a minute, then shot me an apologetic look.

"I'll be there in a few minutes." He clicked off his phone and sighed. "Vehicle ran off the road down on Mayfield, and Mr. Costa wants me to get some shots."

Worry vibrated through me. "Oh my goodness. How bad was the accident?"

His grin had an evil twist to it. "Minor, but it involved the mayor's car."

"You're kidding. It's news because it's the mayor's car?"

He shrugged. "Nothing ever happens around here."

"Except for break-ins and dognapping."

He let out a sigh as he pulled me into his arms. "Would you believe that's the first time since I moved here that anything happened other than minor incidents?"

"So it's me."

He leaned away and studied my face for a moment.

"You aren't serious, right?"

"Not really." I managed a smidgen of a smile. "It's just strange this stuff has happened since I've been here."

"If you're looking for a reason to go back to Jacksonville, let me know. I have a few ideas about how to convince you to stay."

I grinned. "In that case, yes, I'm looking for a reason to leave." I gave him my best wide-eyed innocent look. "Convince me to stay?"

He kissed me for a mind-blowing couple of minutes, then pulled back. "Unfortunately, I have to go right now. Can I convince you later?"

"Oh yeah."

"Remember where we were." He headed toward the bedroom to get dressed.

Meanwhile, the knowledge that he wanted me to stay in Ugly Creek had me feeling all warm inside.

****

Fifteen minutes later, Ace dropped me off at home with a gentle kiss before he headed off to document the mayor's bad day. As I started up the three steps to the front porch, I felt somebody watching me and turned to see Miz Carlisle staring.

"When I was coming up, young ladies didn't butter the bread before it was baked."

She glared darkly at me as I turned and walked across the porch.

I went inside the house, closed the door, and leaned

back against it. "When you were coming up, guys hit young ladies over the head and dragged them back to the man cave."

Terri's laugh came from across the room. "If that crazy old bitch keeps on, she'll drive us to do something useful, like duct taping her mouth."

I sighed. "That sounds entirely too appealing."

"There's some of the sticky stuff under the sink. It's the plain old gray though. Do you think she'd prefer polka-dots? Or maybe something in a nice pastel stripe?"

I laughed so hard I thought I was going to pee my panties. When I finally stopped, Terri grinned at me.

"Feel better?"

"Yes, much." I wiped my eyes as I looked at her. "We have way too little fun at her expense."

"Hell, yes. We must correct that immediately, or at least as soon as I get back from the library." She picked up her computer case."

"You're going out to write?"

"No. I'm dragging my laptop with me because I want to build up my biceps."

"And they say writers don't get enough exercise."

She stuck her tongue out, then started toward the door, only to stop halfway and look back. "Have you told Ace about me?"

Her heartfelt expression surprised me. "The shapeshifting? No."

"If you're getting serious about him, you need to tell him. He's smart, he'll figure it out before long anyway." Her eyes sent concern in my direction. "I wouldn't want my split personality to cause a problem between the two of you."

"We aren't serious."

"Right. You just keep on telling yourself that." She edged past me and out the front door.

I locked the door behind her and headed for the shower. It was good to be alone for a while. Peace and quiet, that's what I'd wanted for a long time. Just being by myself and not having to look after anybody except me.

So why did I feel so restless?

****

I took advantage of the quiet to write, or at least I tried. Unfortunately, I kept getting sidetracked thinking about the man whose bed I'd left only a few hours ago. I told myself it was simple lust coupled with the uncommon feeling of being cared for. I was lying to myself, and I knew it. I was in love. How could I be so stupid as to give a piece of my heart away? Giving to others was all I'd done for most of my life. I needed to take care of me for once.

Besides, a relationship between Ace and me could not possibly work out. He wasn't likely to be interested in something serious, and even if he was, I couldn't take the chance that Mom might need me. I was all she had, and I had to be there for her. I needed to enjoy my freedom while I had it and stop obsessing over a freaking man.

So I forced myself to get back to work. I made progress too, on the contracted book. I was feeling quite proud of myself. Then my cell phone rang.

When I saw the display, I almost put the phone down and ran out the door. I'm a responsible adult, though, so I ignored the mean little voice in my head telling me the fun was over, and answered the cell.

"Hello, sweetheart," Aunt Ruth said. "How are things in Ugly Creek?"

"They're fine here. How's the cruise going?"

"It's fabulous. We're having a wonderful time."

"Is Mom okay?"

"Why don't you talk to her yourself?"

There was the sound of the phone being transferred, and then, "Hello, Shay."

"Mom." Tears stung my eyes. "How are you doing?"

"I'm having a ball." The voice was familiar, the happiness wasn't. "I got hit on by a man not much older than you. Do you believe it? Did wonders for my ego."

Younger man? This had to be an alternate reality or something. "I'm glad you're having a good time."

"How are things going with you?"

"Really well. It's fun living with Terri."

"I'm so glad. I know things have been hard for you, baby. I'm really sorry about that."

"It's okay."

"No, it isn't. I can't change the past, but I can make sure your future is better."

"Mom." My voice cracked.

"Well, I'd better get off the phone so we can go and buy more souvenirs. I'll bring you some great things back. Just wait till you see. Love you, baby."

"Love you too, Mom."

I clicked off the phone, put it down on the table, and stared at it. What the hell had just happened? Who was that happy woman with my mother's voice?

****

I spent sundown sitting on the back steps thinking about my life. Terri was in bed so she could get up and write before daylight. She told me she'd had a call from her mother also, who, like my mom, reported having a wonderful time. Things were working out the way I'd hoped. Why did something still seem off?

My phone sounded and I admit to being a bit startled. Okay, I came close to falling off the steps. Then I saw the name and smiled. "Hi, Ace."

"Hello, beautiful."

My face went warm, and my smile widened. "How did the accident coverage go?"

His warm chuckle sent tingles through me.

"It was crazier than I thought it might be. The mayor's thirteen-year-old daughter was out joyriding with her ten-year-old brother."

Several horrible possibilities shot through my mind. "Oh my God! Are they all right?"

"They're fine, sweetheart. They actually were pretty smart. They stayed on the side roads and wore their seat belts and didn't go very fast. Their ride finally ended when the girl swerved to avoid hitting a squirrel and the car went into a ditch. They couldn't get the car back out, so they called Daddy."

"They weren't hurt? You're sure?"

"I'm sure. They were more afraid of getting in trouble than anything.

The humor in the situation finally got into my head, and I laughed. "Ugly Creek is an odd town, but it's all Southern."

"That it is. Give me your email addy, and I'll send you some pics as soon as I get them downloaded from my camera."

"Thanks."

"How was your afternoon?"

His deep, warm voice did something to my insides, and I heard myself saying, "My mom called."

"Is she enjoying her trip?"

"She says she's having a great time. She definitely sounds happy."

"So nothing's wrong?"

"No. Why?"

"Because you sound down."

"I'm not. I'm happy for her. I am."

"But?"

"I gave up so much for her." I hung my head. What was my problem? "I shouldn't have said that." Tears burned my eyes.

"It's me, honey. You can be open with me."

"But it isn't Mom's fault." Tears escaped and ran down one cheek.

"Hey, don't beat yourself up. Logic doesn't change the way we feel. You about your mother, or me about my parents blaming me for my brother's death."

Shock vibrated through me. "Oh, my God."

"They know it isn't logical. They try to not feel they way they do, but it's hard. I blame myself sometimes too."

"How in the world could you be responsible for your brother's death?"

He was quiet for a minute. "I got mad about something, I don't remember what, and I ran away. Adam went looking for me. It started raining and he got soaked. Two weeks later he was diagnosed with a rare brain tumor."

"You don't get brain tumors from being rained on."

"I know it isn't logical, but when you lose somebody you love, you need somebody to blame."

"You know you aren't responsible, right?"

"Mostly I do. It took me a long time to get there, but I did."

My heart cracked a little. "Oh, Ace." The nickname felt strange given the topic of discussion. "I know your name is Alexander C. Ellison. Have you always gone by your initials?"

He chuckled, which made me feel better.

"My family calls me Alex. How about you, Shannon?"

I laughed. "Clearly we've Googled each other. Pretty much everybody calls me Shay. When we were little, Terri heard somebody say my name was Shannon May, so she ran the two together and called me Shay. It stuck."

"It's cute. I think Shannon is pretty though."

"Thank you." I smiled. My real name on his tongue had me feeling a connection to him I didn't want to examine too closely.

"I'd better go download those shots and send a few to Mr. Costa for tomorrow's paper."

"I should get some word count done before it gets too late."

"Good night, Shannon."

"Good night, Alex."

We hung up, and I sat on the steps a while longer thinking about a future that was not likely to happen. But one I wanted just the same.

Chapter 15

I was awakened the next morning by the sound of rain pouring from the skies punctuated by an occasional clap of thunder. I pulled the blanket over my head. I'm a writer, not a duck. Writers are artistic types, and we don't keep regular hours. Besides, I didn't have anybody to take care of, or watch out for, so I didn't have to get up. If I wanted to I could just stay in bed all day. That thought was so depressing I threw back the covers and got my rear out of that bed.

What was wrong with me? Here I had what I'd wanted for years. Why wasn't I happy? Thoroughly disgusted with myself, I headed to the bathroom. This day was going to start whether I wanted it to or not.

I stumbled into the kitchen just as Trixie blew in through the doggie door. The next thing I knew, the big dog shook water all over the place, followed closely by a naked Terri shaking out her long blonde hair.

"That is so weird."

She looked at me, head tipped to one side.

"What's weird?"

"Your hair being wet. Freaks me out a little every time."

Her forehead wrinkled. "Why?"

"I don't know, it just does." I shrugged.

She shrugged back and headed for her room.

I put coffee in the machine and hoped the storm

would end soon.

****

Three hours and fifteen hundred words later, the storm had ended and I felt good about my work for a change. I was getting close to finishing my contracted book. Then I would be free to go in a new direction if I wanted. The question was, what did I really want?

My cell chirped and a hopeful shiver shot through me, but it wasn't him. "Hello, Stephie."

"Hi, Shay. Did you hear about the rezoning meeting?"

"What rezoning meeting?"

"They're trying to zone your neighborhood so you can't have any type of business."

My breath caught. "Like animal rescues."

"Exactamundo."

"Oh boy. When is this meeting?"

"Thursday night, 7 p.m. Thought you should know."

"Thanks."

"No problem."

I ended that call and immediately dialed another.

"Yeah."

I blinked. "Ace, it's me. Do you know about the rezoning meeting?"

"Oh course I know."

His sharp tone took me by surprise.

"I've spent all morning doing research and making phone calls."

"What can I do to help?"

There was silence for a moment, then a groan. "Ah, sweetheart, I'm sorry. This zoning thing just has me so stressed out I can't think straight. You're supporting me. That means more than you know."

"If I can do anything else, let me know."

"Thank you, honey."

"I know you need to get back to preparing for the meeting. I'll go, but call if you need me."

"Thank you, Shay. You mean a lot to me."

"You mean a lot to me too."

We said our goodbyes, and I leaned back in my desk chair. Who was trying to run Ace out of town? If it was really just Miz Carlisle and maybe a couple of other people, like Mr. Vanetti, it wouldn't happen. Would it?

I'm sure Ace had things well in hand, but it wouldn't hurt for me to poke around a little and talk to a few people. I opened the Internet and searched the town's website. While I was reading that, I dialed Mr. Costa's number. If anybody in this town knew what was going on it was him.

Even Mr. Costa hadn't heard about the zoning change request. The town was so quiet and uneventful that few people seemed to pay attention to what happened at the council meetings.

"They're so boring I only make my reporter stay ten minutes," Mr. Costa said. "If it's going to be one of those rare times something will happen, everybody usually knows about it weeks in advance."

This time, though, the Ugly Creek grapevine was lacking in information. He agreed to put a piece in the paper, and I hurriedly wrote it for him.

I quickly discovered most people knew nothing about the meeting. When I told Stephie that, she and Jake vowed to call everybody they knew. Liza tore herself from business woes long enough to call people.

Even Steve said he'd be at the meeting to back Ace. I was proud of my new friends and how they were willing to come together to protect one of their own.

Tired but filled with pride in my new home, I went out on the porch with a new writers' magazine and braved the Wrath of Carlisle to read on my own front porch. For a while, she made a point of letting me know she was there. Maybe I was boring, because she finally went into her house.

I was reading about contract clauses to look out for, when I heard a voice. I looked up to see Chuck Vanetti walking down the road. He went to the door across the street, and spoke to the man who answered.

Next he crossed to Miz Carlisle's house, but when he saw me he yelled, "Have you seen my dog?"

I put the magazine down and walked over to the fence. The man's forehead was tight and anger flashed in his eyes. "Your dog's missing?" I asked.

"It was that Ellison boy." Miz Carlisle came out and stood with her arms crossed, an expression of disgust on her face.

"No," I said. "It was probably the dognapper."

"There's no dognapper," Miz Carlisle said. "It's that Ellison boy stealing dogs. He's not right in the head."

Mr. Vanetti glared at me. "You were the one with him when he came around messing with my dog."

"He was trying to save your dog's life." I glared right back.

"I can take care of my own damn dog."

"Apparently not," I told him.

He took a step toward me. "I don't like people messing in my business."

I managed to stay where I was and not run like a bunny from a wolf. "Letting a dog die while tied up in your front yard is everybody's business, or should be."

"She's been around that crazy Ellison so much she's starting to sound like him," Miz Carlisle said.

I sucked in my breath. All at once I got it. I understood why Ace felt the way he did. Helpless animals didn't deserve to be mistreated by humans who should know better. "Thank you," I said.

"Where did he put my dog?"

Mr. Vanetti took another step toward me.

"The dognapper took him." I stood and faced the man. Looked him right in the eye.

"She just told you Ellison has him," Miz Carlisle said.

I turned to face the woman. "Ace is not a dognapper. In fact, he's tried hard to find the dogs and discover who took them."

"What do you expect him to do, admit he stole them?"

Miz Carlisle glared right back at me.

I turned to Mr. Vanetti. "Ace will help you find your dog."

He put one hand on the fence and leaned over it until his face was inches from me. "I don't want his help. Or yours."

In spite of using every bit of courage I had, my feet backed a step closer to the edge of the porch. "Your loss."

His eyes widened. "Screw you, I'm going to look for my mutt."

"I'll call the cops for you," Miz Carlisle said.

"Thank you." He headed toward the road.

I turned to go back to the house. For a small, quiet town with a reputation for taking care of each other, this place was nuts.

"I guess you'll just have to go with Ellison when he leaves."

My very last nerve snapped, and I spun to march back to the fence. "Ace is not leaving."

She smiled, but it looked more like a grimace. Seems she rarely exercised those particular facial muscles.

"I wouldn't be so sure if I were you."

I grabbed my magazine from the porch and got myself in the house before I did something I'd regret. Like punch a much older woman in the nose. As soon as I was behind the closed door, I dialed Ace's number. It rang and rang and went to voicemail. "Call me. It's important," I said, then clicked off the phone.

"You okay?"

Terri's frown reminded me I still shook with anger.

"That mean old biddy needs to have an attitude adjustment."

Terri's lips pulled into a mischievous smile. "So, tonight?"

In spite of the state of my emotions, I smiled too. "Seems to be the perfect time."

My cousin chuckled evilly as she headed into the kitchen. To eat, no doubt. If she wasn't a dog, she'd weigh a ton.

I tried Ace's number again. He still wasn't answering. "Vanetti's dog is missing and they're blaming you." I told his voicemail, and hoped he got the message.

Right now I had a plan to pull off.

****

It was that time of day when daylight and dark blend in a colorful, shadowy world where perception is skewed, and confusion is easier to achieve. Or at least that was our working theory.

Trixie bounced out the doggie door and loped around the yard a couple of times. When she came close to the back porch where I could see her, she met my gaze and lowered her head in a nod. I nodded back and slipped around the corner of Aunt Ruth's house, using the small bushes across the front of the house to obscure my movements. I got in what I hoped was a good position, made sure my little camera was ready, and waited for the show to begin.

Miz Carlisle, puttering in her flowerbed as usual, couldn't miss seeing Trixie leap over the fence into her yard. If that hadn't attracted her attention, Bumpkins's high-pitched yowl would have done the trick.

The woman got to her feet faster than a person of her age should be able to, and rushed toward Trixie. "Get out of here, you big smelly menace!"

I used the distraction to move closer, ducking behind the shrubs on her side of the fence to get into position for part two.

Trixie vanished into the shadows near the back of the house. Bumpkins edged that way, stopping to hiss every few feet.

"It's all right," Miz Carlisle told the cat. "I'll make sure that mean old doggie doesn't hurt you."

She turned toward the back of the house, chin up, fists clenched. I raised my camera to catch her next reaction. It didn't take long. Miz Carlisle screamed, and I caught the moment for posterity.

"What are you doing in my yard like that?" The old woman made an up-and-down motion with her hand.

Terri stood smiling at the woman and her cat. "I came over to play with Bumpkins." She reached her hand out toward the cat, and he backed away.

The side of the cat's body was against Miz C's legs, his fur stood on end, and he hissed with everything he had.

"Leave him alone!" Miz C. yelled. "Where is that mangy mutt of yours? He was in my yard getting Bumpkins all stirred up."

"Trixie wasn't out here. *She's* home taking a nap."

"You're lying. I saw the beast, and Bumpkins did too."

Terri squatted in front of the cat and proceeded to baby talk to him. "Did you see the big, pretty doggie? She'd like to play with you."

Bumpkins backed away, still hissing, until he was behind Miz C and glaring at Terri from between his human's legs.

"Dogs and cats don't play together." The woman leaned away, her lip curled, and her hand on her throat, as if Terri had just suggested she try a particularly kinky sexual position.

I was about to begin my part of the party when a car pulling into Miz C's driveway brought the festivities to an abrupt halt.

Miz C glanced at the car and then back at Terri. "Get out of here before I call the cops. Nudity is illegal, you know."

"Only in public," Terri muttered as she slipped into the foliage

The car's door opened and a man stepped out.

"What are you doing here?" Miz C asked.

"Nice to see you too, Mama."

"What do you want?" the woman glanced toward where Terri had been, and her eyes widened. "I told her that mangy beast was in my yard!"

Trixie paused when she passed me behind Miz C's shrubs. I'd seen it before, but a collie winking at me will still be a weird experience when I'm as old as dirt. Like having a cousin who can morph into a dog isn't strange enough.

"What a beautiful collie," the man said, as he reached his hand out to Trixie.

She sat in front of him, giving him her best I'm-a-sweet-doggie look. He scratched her head, and she looked up at him with great affection.

"Don't touch that horrible beast."

"Chill, Mom, dogs are amazing animals."

"They're nasty."

The man sighed. "No more so than cats."

Using the subsequent heated argument as a distraction, I headed back toward the house before I was spotted. Trixie could hold her own.

I was almost at the porch when Ace's car pulled into our driveway. "Welcome to Grand Central Station," I muttered, wondering what happened to our carefully laid plan. By the time Ace slid out of his Xterra, though, I was smiling.

"Hello, Shay. Sorry to just stop by, but you weren't answering your phone."

I'd left it in the house to make sure some unexpected noise didn't screw up our plan. "Welcome to my world."

He tugged me closer for a quick, hot kiss.

"I stopped by to thank you."

"Thank me for what?"

He leaned closer and whispered in my ear.

"For the heads up. I was able to get Buster to a friend."

A sharp chill moved through me. "You took Vanetti's dog."

Wariness flashed in his eyes.

He edged us right up against the side of his SUV and leaned close.

"I was trying to save him."

A horrible question twisted my heart. "Were you trying to save the others too?"

"You think I took the other dogs?" Disappointment weighed down the words. "I thought you knew me better than that."

Pain twisted my heart. "You stole a dog."

"Yes, I did."

I started to speak, but he held up a hand.

"Buster's chain was wrapped around that damn tree again. He couldn't have reached his water bowl. Not that it mattered; there was no water in it anyway."

My accusing heart felt heavy in my chest. What was I thinking? Ace wasn't a thief, he was a hero. "You saved his life."

He didn't say anything as I stood there trying to deal with the emotions filling my throat. Finally I was able to look at him. "I'm sorry, Alex."

His lips pulled into a soft smile. "You're a special woman, Shannon."

Warm tingles invaded my stomach and spread throughout my body from there. Time stood still as we looked into each other's eyes. Until the sound of a big dog jumping over the fence broke the enchantment. Trixie headed our way, looked me straight in the eye, and barked once sharply.

"Something important?" I asked.

She dipped her head once, then headed around the house.

I turned back to Ace, who was giving me a very strange look.

"I guess you're wondering what that was all about."

He looked at me like he was trying to decide which of us needed the straightjacket more.

"You were talking to the dog."

"Yes."

He licked his lips and I saw the hint of a smile.

"And she answered?"

"Yes." I put a hand on his arm. "Trixie is not your average dog."

"She's very well-trained. Your cousin should be proud."

I hated to deflate his belief all this was normal. "Let's go in the house and see what she found out that's so important."

"You're kidding, right?"

I took his hand and tugged him toward the porch steps. "Come on. It'll be okay."

Terri, wearing a robe, met us in the living room.

"What did you find out?" I asked, as I shoved Ace toward a chair.

"Wait," he said. "It was Trixie who supposedly found something out." He narrowed his eyes. "You have a recorder on the dog, don't you? Not a bad idea."

"No," I said. "No recorder. Trixie heard something

important."

"The dognapper is Agent Max Killian," Terri said.

Sharp little shocks skittered down my arms and legs. "The FBI agent?"

"Yep."

"This is ridiculous." Ace, still standing, crossed his arms over his chest. "And way too important to play games."

"It's not a game, Ace. Trixie really was spying on our neighbor."

"How could you possibly know what the damn dog heard?" He looked at Terri. "Let me guess, you're psychic."

"No. I'm Trixie."

Ace groaned. "You're a human, not a dog."

"She's both," I said.

"This is not funny."

He gave me a hard glare.

"I'll show you," Terri said.

He turned to look at her. "Right, and I'll—"

Where Trixie had been standing was a collie with a bathrobe hanging over her back.

"What the hell?"

He stumbled, and I edged him into the nearest chair. Out of the corner of my eye, I saw Trixie head for Terri's room.

"Did she really just do that?"

"Yes, she did."

"I was afraid you were gonna say that."

"This from the man who's friends with Bigfoot."

"Bigfoot is an unusual creature, that's all. This is…crazy."

"When you two finish discussing metaphysical

possibilities, I'd like to figure out what to do about this dognapper-agent dude." Terri strode into the room and sat on the edge of the coffee table. She was wearing shorts and a halter top.

"Thanks for getting dressed," I said.

Ace looked at her as if he were afraid she'd morph into a gator or something. I enjoyed his expression for a moment before reality lowered its weight back into my thoughts. I swallowed. "It's not just taking the dogs, you know. Killian is investigating Steve's break-in."

Terri's eyes widened. "Do you think it's possible the two are related?"

"How could they not be?"

We both turned to look at Ace, and he shrugged.

"Unless you believe it's a coincidence that the napping and investigation happened simultaneously and with the same man involved in both."

"Maybe he was here for the investigation and decided it was a great opportunity to steal dogs." Terri's face was pale.

"Or the investigation was a setup to cover the dognapping."

I shuddered. "By that logic he must be involved in the software theft."

Ace nodded slowly. "It's possible."

Terri sighed. "Oh, boy."

Something occurred to me. "Wait a minute. How did you find this out over in Miz Carlisle's yard? Is her son involved?"

"No," Terri said. "She is."

Chapter 16

"Miz C is involved in dognapping?" I couldn't wrap my head around it.

Terri nodded. "She got a call on her cell phone. I didn't even know she had a cell, did you? Anyway the caller was Agent Killian and they were discussing whether they had enough dogs."

"You're sure about this?" Ace asked.

"Positive," Terri said.

"Her son must be involved too," Ace said. "If she was talking right in front of him."

"No, I don't think so. She moved almost to the house to take the call." Terri grinned. "Only a dog could have heard what was said from that far away."

"What do we do?" I asked, still thrown by our elderly neighbor being somehow involved with a dog-stealing FBI agent.

"The first thing I'm going to do is call Steve." Ace pulled out his phone.

"Are you sure that's a good idea?" Terri leaned forward in her seat. "Not about warning him, about using a cell to do it. This Killian dude is FBI."

Ace groaned. "I should have thought of that."

"Don't worry," I said. "She's a very smart doggie."

"Bite me." Terri narrowed her eyes.

"He's probably still at work. I'll—"

He was interrupted by loud knocking at our door.

"I know you're in there, Ellison. I see your mutt-mobile out here," Vanetti's voice boomed from the porch.

"We'll distract him; you go out the back." Terri was on her feet and ready for action.

"Thanks, but no," Ace said. "I have to face him eventually."

"Are you sure?" I asked, hoping he saw my understanding of his dilemma.

"Yeah, I'm sure," he said. He took a deep breath, then went to the door and jerked it open. "What do you want?"

"Where's my dog?"

"How should I know?"

"Because you stole him."

"You do know there's a dognapper, right?"

"I know you're crazy."

"Takes one to know one," Terri muttered.

Vanetti glared at Ace." Hiding behind two women." He shook his head. "You need to grow a pair."

Ace reached for his zipper. "Want to compare?"

Vanetti's eyes widened. He turned and all but ran off the porch and through the yard.

Terri chuckled. "I'll bet it would take three little blue pills and two hookers to get his little Vanetti into action."

Okay, that surprised me. When I looked toward her, she shrugged.

Ace took my hands in his.

"I have to warn Steve," he said.

"Be careful out there."

"I will."

He gave me a warm little kiss that held promise for

later and turned toward his Xterra.

I watched his taillights until Terri put her arm around me. "Let's go in. I'm in the mood for a strategy session."

As I went for the door, I caught a glimpse of Miz C leaning on the white fence, a smug smile on her face.

I sighed. I moved here to figure out who I am and where I go from here. I expected Ugly Creek to be a quiet, relaxing little town. What I got was convoluted, odd, and complicated.

I really should not be enjoying myself.

****

"It's too dangerous."

Ace, Terri, and I gathered around our tiny kitchen table planning The Great Dognapper Sting.

Terri touched the pink dog collar around her neck. "I have a GPS. You can't lose me."

"But you can't tell us if you get into trouble," I pointed out.

"What if the collar falls off? Or he finds it?" Ace asked.

"Trixie can take care of herself."

Ace's face was tight with obvious worry. "Trixie is a dog."

Terri gave him a look similar to a mother trying to explain to a two-year-old why he can't have a pony in the house. For the forty-seventh time. "She doesn't have to be."

"Sure," I said. "A naked woman with no weapon and no phone is so much better."

Terri grinned. "Trust me, honey, I can borrow a phone. And anything can be a weapon."

"I still don't like it," I told her.

"Me either," Ace said.

"Anybody have a better idea?"

Ace and I looked at each other. She was right; her plan was our best shot at nailing the disgusting piece of gnat crap and getting the animals back to their families.

"That's what I thought."

She crossed her arms and looked first at one, then the other of us.

"How about we get this show on the road."

A few minutes later Ace and I sat on his porch and watched my laptop screen. On it was the GPS output from Trixie's collar. It was growing later and later in the afternoon. The GPS showed Trixie going up one street then down the other, slowly circling the town. I was glad she was safe, but frustrated too. Maybe our plan wouldn't work.

"You did say that most of the dogs were taken in the early to late afternoon, correct?"

"Yes," Ace said. "Actually, all of them that I know about."

"You think there are others?"

He shrugged. "I have no idea. It's not like people report to me."

"They should."

His smile and the mischief flashing in his eyes warmed my heart. "Why should they report to me?"

"Because I said so."

He chuckled as he leaned in for a kiss. For a moment I was lost in the magic of Ace's arms. Then I caught a glimpse of the computer screen and shoved him away. "She's stopped."

He studied the screen for a moment, then turned to me. "Let's go."

I nodded, grabbed my laptop, and we headed for his Xterra.

It took maybe three minutes to get to the intersection where Trixie's signal had stopped.

"I don't see her," Ace said.

"The GPS says she's that way." I pointed to the woods.

He drove the Xterra around the corner, where he pulled off the road. "That's an odd place for a plumbing truck."

Sure enough a generic white "Bill's Plumbing" truck was parked in front of a vacant lot next to Miz Funderburk's house.

"I've never heard of a "Bill's Plumbing"," I said.

"Me either."

Just then, a familiar collie came bounding out of the woods, zigzagging from one side to the other. FBI Agent Killian ran after the dog as she twisted and turned through the cat woman's yard, even at one point circling around Killian, then barking until he turned and chased after her again.

Ace grinned. "I believe our girl is leading the dognapper on a merry chase."

I enjoyed the show myself. "Should we wait until she wears him out?"

He laughed. "I think she's pretty much done that."

Trixie took Killian through a convoluted series of movements that made me tired just watching. Even from where we sat, I could tell he was getting tired. He slipped and barely stopped himself from hitting the ground. She seemed to kick up the pressure after that, and sure enough, Kilian slipped and face-planted. Trixie dove onto his back, front paws on his shoulders, holding him down.

"That's our cue," I said, then realized Ace was already out of the car. I dove out and headed after him, running in an attempt to catch up.

"Get that pooch off me," the agent pleaded.

"Why would I do that?" Ace asked.

Trixie gave him a doggie smile.

Ace turned to me. "You call the police and I'll see what's in the truck."

"No need. I already called the cops."

We turned to see Miz Funderburk standing near us, cell phone in hand.

"So this is the tree slime that's been snatching the poor dogs."

"I thought you liked cats," Killian commented, his voice gaining him a growl from Trixie.

"You tell him, girl," Miz Funderburk said. "And for your information, cats are my favorite, but I love all animals."

I realized Ace wasn't beside me. He opened the door of the plumbing van. Dogs barked and my heart went into my throat. "Bastard," I muttered.

Trixie barked agreement.

"I agree," Miz Funderburk said, as she kicked one of Killian's legs.

"Ow!"

Trixie growled and he shut up.

A police car pulled up, and Ken Bennett got out. Relief washed over me at the sight of Ace's friend.

"So this is the dognapper," Ken said, as he walked up. When he got a good look at the guy Trixie was holding down, he stopped in his tracks. "Agent Killian, is that you?"

"Yes, and get this mutt off of me."

Trixie growled and Ken's lips twitched. He looked at Trixie. "I'll cuff him if you'll move." She backed off, and he straddled Killian and pulled his arms back to cuff him.

"What are you doing? You can't arrest me. I'm a frigging FBI agent and these folks are nuts."

"He chased that beautiful collie," Miz Funderburk said. "He tried to give her a pork chop, but she didn't want it. She's smart, that meat was probably drugged."

"I don't know what she's talking about." Killian shifted his head so he could look up at Ken. "She's that crazy cat woman, you know."

Trixie gave a low growl.

"That mutt is a menace," Killian said. "It's going to hurt somebody. Like me."

Trixie's quick bark sounded a lot like a laugh.

Ken glanced at her then shook his head. "You'd better worry about your own problems, Killian."

Ken pulled his prisoner to his feet, then looked from Miz Funderburk to me. "I'll need a statement from each of you, and Ace."

"I'll tell him," I told the cop.

The agent laughed. "So I grabbed a few dogs. I was trying to help them."

I stepped toward him. "Help them? They didn't need help."

"How do you know? Maybe they were being treated awful. They'd go to a good home. That's what your boyfriend does, isn't it?"

"Ace doesn't steal dogs from perfectly good homes for some nefarious reason." I took another step toward him. "What were you doing with the dogs anyway?"

"That's a really good question," Ken said. "I'm sure the answer involves money."

Killian shrugged. "Yeah, some. Mostly I was doing it to help out my nephew."

"How does stealing dogs help your nephew?" Miz Funderburk asked.

Trixie barked.

"He's starting a little dog business. The mutts really would go to a good home."

I fought the urge to strangle the jerk. "Why not get the dogs from a shelter? There are plenty of animals who need good homes."

"Costs money, and you never know what crap those mutts have."

"So you take dogs from little boys." The very thought shot tremors of anger and disgust through my body. This was surreal. A federal agent grabbing pets to be sold by a relative. What a loathsome man.

"I'll get a statement from the three of you tomorrow." Ken grabbed the man's arm and pulled him toward where the police car was parked. "Let's go, Killian."

The agent's smiled smugly. "I'll get a slap on the wrist and go back to my job. I only took animals. Who cares what happens to them?"

I didn't think. I never considered repercussions. I didn't plan. I just acted. My right fist hit Killian's face. My hand ached but my brain barely recognized the pain. He stumbled into Ken, who shoved him back up. Only then did it occur to me I'd assaulted a federal agent.

"Did you see that?" Killian's eyes bulged.

"See what?" Ken asked, as he jerked his prisoner in

the direction of the police car.

The dognapper still yapped as he was taken away. Ken was shoving the man into his car, when he looked toward me and winked. Relieved, and mystified, I watched until the cruiser went around the corner.

Ace stood next to Miz Funderburk, his arm around her shoulders. "I'm glad you're getting some help. I've been worried about you," Ace said to her.

"Are you all right?" I asked her.

"I'm doing better. I was just telling Ace that people have been coming by with food and insisting on helping me clean up. Plus, my nephew is coming here next week to stay with me for a while and help me get my house straightened out." She sighed. "My daughter tries to help, but she believes the only way to do it is to take everything out all at once. She thinks it's all junk, but my things mean a lot to me." She sniffled. "My nephew Landon understands. He's a psychologist who works with hoarders like me. He's been planning to come for a while, but between things he had to do, and Lexi's bullheaded insistence that hers was the only possible way to do things…" She closed her eyes.

"Your nephew will help you." I cringed inwardly at the pathetic sentiment, but it was all I had at the moment.

She smiled. "He will."

"I'm glad." I looked for my cousin, and saw Trixie nearby, bonding with the cutest fluffy white kitten I'd ever seen.

"Are the dogs okay?" I asked Ace.

"They seem to be," he answered. "Animal control is on the way. I called a vet I know, but I'm not sure she'll get here before they do."

"You don't trust animal control." It wasn't a question. I knew how he felt.

"Why would he?" Miz Funderburk asked. "The men who work for them are mostly jerks who don't care about animals. They're just doing what they do for the money."

"And the less they have to work, the better they like it," Ace said.

"No women?"

Both of them shook their heads. "Nary a one," Miz F. said. "Women tend to be more compassionate. Can't have that."

Ace's features tightened. "Plus, there are no Vanetti females old enough to work for them."

I swallowed. "So that really is how Chuck Vanetti gets away with so much."

"Yep."

I closed my eyes and thought about that poor, mistreated dog. Ace saved lives. They just weren't human lives. When I looked at him, he smiled my way. He still had his arm around Miz F, comforting her, supporting her, understanding her. He wasn't a dog person, he was an underdog person. Right then and there, my heart melted and the tiny part of the organ I'd been holding back flew over and offered itself to him.

The sound of the animal control vehicle interrupted my train of thought, but I knew things would never be the same.

Chapter 17

As soon as we walked in the door, Trixie trotted off toward the bathroom.

I sighed. "What a day."

"You aren't kidding," Ace said.

"But we got the bad guy."

Ace rubbed his forehead. "You, me, Cat Woman, and your cousin the dog."

I shrugged. "It worked.

"I still can't wrap my head around that whole Terri and Trixie thing. Even after seeing her change, my brain doesn't want to believe it."

"I've known her literally all my life, and sometimes the thought of what she is blows my mind." I put my hand on his arm. "Are you hungry?"

"Actually, I should be getting home. Check on the dogs. Do some thinking."

Why wasn't he looking at me? "I understand," I told him, but I didn't.

"See you later."

He touched his lips to my forehead, then still not looking at me, he turned and walked out the door.

I locked the door behind him and leaned my head against the wood. Had my worry he'd run if he knew Terri's secret shot me straight into the very situation I was trying to avoid?

"Where's Ace?" Terri stood in the middle of the

room, barefoot and wearing her Snoopy pajamas.

"He went home to check on things. And think."

"I'm sorry." Her voice was almost a whisper.

"It's not your fault." I collapsed on the couch.

She slid in beside me. "What I am scares him."

"He lives in Ugly Creek. He knows Bigfoot."

She put a hand on my shoulder. "It's different when you watch somebody you know change into something else."

The look on her face sent tingles to my stomach. I aimed for a teasing tone. "What would you know about that?"

She picked at an invisible piece of lint on her leg. "I saw my dad shift."

I knew I was staring, but I couldn't stop. "I thought your dad left just after you were born."

"That's what Mom tells people. I think that's what she wants to believe, but the truth is I was almost four when he left."

"I knew he was where the shifter gene came from, but you actually saw him shift. Wow."

"It was freaky. Seriously freaky." She twisted so she faced me, propped her elbow on the back of the couch, and rested her head on her hand. "It was maybe a week before my fourth birthday, but it seemed like it'd never get here." She grinned, but the expression faded fast into sadness. "I was supposed to be napping in my room, but I saw Daddy through the window and decided I wanted to go out there with him." She looked down, the muscles in her jaw jumping like she was fighting to get the words out.

I put my hand on her shoulder. "It's just you and me, and I love you like a sister."

She nodded. "As I was crossing the lawn, I saw this huge lizard, or at least it seemed huge to a four-year-old. I think it might have been an iguana, but back then all I knew was that I was scared of the thing."

She gave me a weak smile.

"But I also wanted to chase it around the yard. I caught a glimpse of Daddy and ran toward him."

She looked down for a moment, then took a deep breath. "He was naked, and I'd never seen him, or any other male, naked before. I stood there, confused by how strange he looked. There was a blurring movement, and then a big dog stood where my dad had been. I found out later that he becomes more wolf than collie, but then all I knew was that my Daddy was gone and there was a huge dog looking right at me."

"You must have been terrified." My heart ached for the little girl she had been.

"I was. I screamed and ran hard toward the house. Mom came busting through the front door and grabbed me. She took me in the house, sat in a chair, and held me in her arms. Daddy came in a little later, but I refused to even look at him. I heard Mom and Daddy arguing that night. The next day he was gone."

"I'm so sorry."

She wiped at her eyes. "The point is that seeing something that crazy isn't easy to deal with."

"I'm sorry, Terri."

"I just wish I'd had the courage to ask why he really left." She rubbed the center of her forehead. "Mom's always said he didn't want to be with us anymore, but I think he left because he scared me."

"Then he wasn't much of a father. He could have at least contacted you after you grew up."

She nodded. "You're right."

"Of course I am."

She hugged me. "Ace will deal with my collie-ness. Just give him time."

"Are you sure?"

"Absolutely."

Unfortunately, I knew her well enough to see the worry behind the smile. "Thanks, Terri."

She hugged me again before she got to her feet.

About halfway to her bedroom she stopped. "Miz F knew what I am."

I blinked, trying to think of something other than the obvious. "You mean that you're a shapeshifter?"

She nodded. "I don't know how, but she knew."

"What makes you so sure?"

"She talked to me like I was human."

"A lot of people do that."

Terri shook her head. "There's a difference between the way a human speaks to a human and the way they talk to animals."

"Interesting."

"Then she said it had been a long time since she'd seen one of my kind."

My head went spinning without me. "How could she possibly know?"

She shrugged. "You'd know more about that than I would."

Made sense, I guess, but I'd never thought about what was different about Terri, or Trixie, that would clue me in to the fact she was different. Then it hit me. "Your smell."

Terri's eyes widened. "Excuse me?"

"I don't mean it like that. You know how I'm

always saying you smell vaguely like dog right after you shift back?"

"Yeah, and I should probably be insulted."

"Probably," I bit back the smile that would likely lead to being blasted by loud music every day for the foreseeable future. "The thing is, it never entirely goes away. Now that I think about it, Trixie smells a little like Terri too."

"Makes sense, I guess."

She plopped down beside me.

"So, do I smell like Trixie?"

I did an exaggerated sniffing exploration over her head, face, and shoulders. The girl had just showered, but sure enough, there was a lingering scent of dog. "Yeah, you do."

"In a bad way?"

The worried expression on her face tore at my heart. "No. Just a slight, sweet scent. I'm not even sure I'd recognize it as canine if we hadn't been talking about it. It's stronger right after you shift,

"Hm, glad I don't stink."

"I would never have agreed to spend an entire year with you if you were a stinky mutt."

"Trixie's not a mutt." She hugged me anyway and headed off to bed.

Before I could start thinking about one handsome beach bum and if he'd ever get past the whole doggie-cousin thing, I forced myself up and toward my bed. I had to believe Ace and I could work things out, or I'd probably melt into a puddle of tears. I loved the damn man. I couldn't help myself.

I'd come to Ugly Creek to learn to live without the responsibility of another person. Instead, I was living with an irresponsible shapeshifter and involved with a man who couldn't even keep up with his phone.

I spent the night waking up every few hours wondering how I'd managed to get myself tied up in responsibility all over again.

The sun was coming up when I woke with Ace's words in my head. "You aren't responsible for your cousin's actions." Wasn't that true? Terri and Ace were perfectly capable adults. Neither of them needed me to take care of them.

With this startling insight, I covered up my head and resolved to sleep till noon. That plan only lasted an hour or so when my phone rang. "Hello," I mumbled, my eyes still closed.

"When you get a chance, could you come down here? I'd really like somebody to talk to."

Chapter 18

I pushed open the door to Blackwood Antiques with a stomach full of worry. Stephie was with a customer, but she smiled and mouthed thank you. I wandered around, enjoying the variety of items in their store.

A few minutes later, the woman left, and Stephie headed my way.

"Thanks for coming."

"No problem. What's going on? You sounded upset."

She nodded and indicated the sales counter. "Would you like some coffee first?"

"I'd love some," I told her.

We went over to the counter, and she poured two mugs. "You know about the FBI agent being the dognapper, right?"

"I was there when he was arrested. Let me tell you, he's not a nice man."

Stephie nodded. "I heard you were there, but I don't trust rumors."

"Don't blame you."

She took a deep breath. "Because he's a criminal, all of his work on the break-in at Z-Com Tech is now under suspicion. Even his partner was pulled off the investigation. Two new agents have taken over, and they're basically starting from scratch."

My heart tore and sank to my belly. "Oh no. Poor Steve and Liza!"

"I'm sorry to drag you here. I know I could have told you all this on the phone." Tears filled Stephie's eyes and she blinked them away. "The thing is, Jake went out there, and I stayed to keep the store open. It didn't take long for me to realize I couldn't stand being here by myself."

"Don't feel bad about calling me, Stephie. I'm your friend. Friends are there for each other." I smiled. "Besides, coming here and looking at all the things you have is hardly an imposition. More like a treat."

The sound of the door caught my attention, and I turned to see Aunt Octavia stroll in.

Stephie rushed to hug the gray-haired woman, who wore a bright orange track suit today. They embraced, then Psychic Woman took Stephie's hand and proceeded to rub her finger over Stephie's palm. "Good tidings await you very soon."

Stephie frowned, but said, "Thank you," and hugged Aunt Octavia again.

When the woman turned to me, I forced a smile. "Hello again."

"So you were visited by the wise one. What an honor!"

"Um, wise one?"

A knowing smile pulled at her lips. "She of the golden horn."

My jaw damn near hit my chest. "You mean the unicorn?"

"Such a crass name for so regal and ancient a creature."

She touched her fingers to my cheek.

"You should be honored to have been chosen."

"It said something about me untangling something. Any idea what that means?"

"You will understand at the proper time."

"Thanks. That was so not helpful."

The knowing smile was back. "What fun would it be if we knew everything?"

She turned and was almost at the door, while I stood there looking stupid. Then it hit me. "How did you know I saw a unicorn?"

She turned that knowing smile on me again.

"To those who know what to look for, it's obvious."

With that she walked out the door.

"You saw a unicorn?"

My face went hot and I shrugged. "That's what it looked like."

Stephie chuckled. "Trust me, if it looked like a unicorn, it was a unicorn. This is Ugly Creek, after all."

I dropped into one of the tall stools behind the counter. "What is it with this place?"

She squeezed my shoulder as she walked behind me to perch on the other stool. "There are theories, but nobody really knows why this area seems to exist on some other plane."

"Psychic aunts, unicorns, Bigfoot."

"Faeries, aliens, leprechauns, oh my."

She had to be pulling my leg. "Aliens as in not from this country?"

She slowly shook her head. "Aliens as in not from this planet. Or maybe this reality, I'm not sure how it works."

Wow! "Thank you for opening up about the

creatures around here. Nobody else will tell me anything."

She shrugged. "It wasn't that long ago that I was wondering if I were losing my mind because I was seeing furry critters. Turns out, Bigfoot is the least weird thing you're likely to see."

I started to ask about the faeries, but the opening of the door interrupted me. When Jake walked in, Stephie rushed to him, but it was the man behind him that caught my attention. Ace met my gaze, and I saw him swallow. For a few seconds, we were the only people on earth. Then what Jake was saying sank in.

"The place is swarming with government agents, and they were very clear they didn't want anybody there who wasn't involved with the case. We finally gave up and left."

"I thought they were only sending two other agents." Stephie's face had lost some of its color.

"That's what Steve thought too. There are two who are running the investigation, but they brought an army with them."

"I so want to take a baseball bat to that Killian jerk." Anger roughened Ace's words.

I turned toward him. His mouth was set in a straight line, and his eyes flashed anger like I hadn't seen on him before. "Ace," it came out as a whisper.

"He has no respect for anything or anybody. He kidnaps dogs for profit, and now, because of that, Steve and Liza have to go through more crap." He looked at his feet, his chest rising and falling in a hard rhythm.

My hand touched his arm before I realized what I'd done. His gaze captured mine, and heat moved through me. Great, my friends were falling apart all around me, and my traitorous body was thinking pleasure. "I'll help you," I said. "With the bat."

His lips twitched. "Thanks, but you already had your shot."

I cringed. "Yep, that's me. Punched a federal agent while a cop was holding him. Go me."

He chuckled. "I can see it now, big awesome FBI dude tells the judge how a little redheaded spitfire punched him."

My face went hot. "Well, when you put it like that."

Jake and Stephie were deep in conversation. It was time to go away.

"I'm leaving, you guys," Ace said, before I could get the words out myself. "There's nothing we can do, and I have to get ready for the tar and feathering tonight."

"Can't they change the meeting date?" I asked.

"They could," Jake said, "but they won't."

Ace shook his head. "Carlisle and Vanetti would raise hell"

"We'll be at the meeting," Stephie said, and pulled Ace into a hug.

"Absolutely." Jake shook Ace's hand.

There were goodbyes, and Ace and I walked to the street where both our vehicles were parked.

I was taking my time, wondering what to say, when I realized Ace had stopped. I looked where he was looking, but there didn't seem to be anything there.

"This is a beautiful little town," he said.

"It really is."

"I let myself get too attached, to forget that reality always destroys the dream."

He looked at me.

"I started to believe I could have it all."

My stomach twisted sideways. "What are you talking about?"

He took my hand in his, and I saw tears glistening in those incredible green eyes. "I don't want to leave Ugly Creek."

My heart banged against my ribs so hard my chest hurt. "You won't have to leave."

His somber smile told a story of hurt suffered over years, and it was all I could do not to throw myself into his arms and sob with him until we were both drained. Years of experience kicked in, and I shoved my feelings back into the abyss I'd hidden them in most of my life. "Your friends aren't going to let a couple of sour-hearted old varmints force you away from your home."

"There may not be anything you can do."

An odd tingle rushed through me, and my mouth went on autopilot. "This is Ugly Creek. Anything is possible."

His smile was weak, but I was glad to see it nonetheless.

"You're buying into that?"

I leaned closer to him and whispered, "I saw a unicorn."

His smile widened. "Writers!"

I smiled back. "It's true. I really did see one."

He narrowed his eyes. "You're making that up."

"Nope. Saw her in the woods. Freaked me out."

He was still looking at me with suspicion, so I continued the story. "Aunt Octavia calls them 'wise ones'."

"So you told Aunt Octavia?"

"No. She just looked at me and knew. I asked about what it said, and she told me I'd understand about the untangling when the time is right."

He leaned toward me, some of the connection we'd shared reflected in his face. "The unicorn talked to you?"

"Actually more like ESP, but yeah, it communicated. Between the unicorn and the psychic, they have me totally confused. Apparently I have somebody's house key and I'm supposed to help them untangle their knitting."

Ace chuckled and my heart leaped.

"I doubt that's whatever she, or the unicorn, said is supposed to mean."

I did an exaggerated eye roll. "I suppose Aunt Octavia is right and I'll have to wait until the 'proper time' and then it'll be all clear and stuff."

He wrapped his arms around me.

"Sweetheart, you could almost make me believe in forever."

I was trying to wrap my head around what he'd just said as he touched his lips gently to mine. Then turned and walked away.

Chapter 19

The meeting room was just inside the town hall entrance and took up a good third of the building. Still, most of the seats were filled, and the number of mulling citizens had to far outnumber the few remaining chairs.

I pushed through the mob, determined to find out how Ace was holding up. A familiar voice had me cringing, and I looked toward the source. There was Miz Carlisle, dressed in one of her familiar housedresses, this one white with a pattern of pink and yellow flowers. With her were Vanetti and a couple of middle-age-crabby-looking folks. She pontificated on how things had gone to hell since Ugly Creek had started letting "all kinds" live there.

In an effort to prevent myself from going to jail for smacking an old lady around, I forced myself to focus on looking for Ace.

Toward one side of the room I saw Lily. I smiled, hoping she saw me. Odd, when her gaze briefly touched mine, she turned and spoke to the man next to her. Then she headed out the door without looking my way. A couple of minutes later, the man turned toward the hallway and an alert sounded in my brain. His gaze was down and he wore a ball cap, but I recognized him.

What the hell was Lily Bennett doing with one of the head security guys at Z-Com Tech?

I slipped out of the room to the wide hall in time to

see the man round the corner toward the side exit. I followed slowly, hoping I could get close enough to check out the situation without being seen. I could really use Terri's canine ears, but there was no answer to my text.

I peeked out the glass door and saw Lily and the security dude standing toe-to-toe in a corner formed by the outside wall and some foliage. The shadow of a big tree provided additional cover, making it clear they wanted privacy.

I surreptitiously watched them gaze at each other while I slipped out the door and circled around to a point where I could hear them, but they couldn't see me.

"We need to leave tonight," the security guy said.

"Not just yet." Lily said. "I still have things to arrange."

"What if they figure it out? I could go to jail."

"They won't figure anything out."

"You don't know that."

"It'll be fine, Ronnie."

Lily's low, sexy voice aimed at a man who wasn't her husband made me want to smack her. Ken seemed like a great guy, I couldn't believe his own wife would treat him like that.

"I'd better get going. The more we're together the bigger risk of being seen."

"Go ahead, I need to get back in there and do my bit to support Ace."

A few seconds later Ronnie took off toward the parking lot. Soon after that, Lily came into my sight briefly as she headed back toward the side door.

I edged back into the shadows until I was sure both

of them were long gone, then strolled around the building toward the front. As I went, I pulled my cell from my pocket. The phone had vibrated while I watched Lily and friend and I couldn't check it. I wasn't surprised the text was from Terri, or that I saw my cousin heading toward me from the direction of the parking lot.

As soon as she got close, she asked, "Did you need something?"

"I could have used Sleuth Dog's super hearing, but I managed with stealthy spying."

She frowned. "What's up?"

"Long story. Let's go let Ace know we're here for him, and I'll explain later."

"Sounds like a plan."

She wrapped her arm around my shoulders.

"Let's go support our Ace."

I wanted to say *my* Ace, but that was silly.

Terri, with her canine senses, had no problem heading directly to the man of the hour. He sat in the front row surrounded by some people I didn't know and several I did, including Jake and Stephie.

Terri hugged him.

"Thanks for being here," he told her.

When she moved back, his gaze met mine. He stood and pulled me into his arms. "I'm so glad you're here."

"I wouldn't be anywhere else."

He kept hold of me as he turned back to his seat, where the spot beside him magically opened for me. He spoke with the people around him, but he never let go of my hand.

A few minutes later, newly appointed Mayor

Sophie Paradise called the meeting to order. For almost two hours, ordinary business was discussed. Then the topic the crowd had been waiting for came up for discussion: the zoning change.

The proposal was read then Miz Carlisle spoke. "Ugly Creek is a quiet place because we've always been selective about the type of people we allow to live in this town. Outsiders have always been required to meet our standards before they were allowed to join our community. Sadly, over the last few years our little town seems to have stopped expecting perspective new citizens to meet those traditional standards. As an example, Ace Ellison was allowed to move into our community and with him has come a plague of loud, nasty, dangerous mutts. His home is overrun with these animals, and they frequently find their way into the community. These filthy creatures represent both a blight on our community, and a very real danger to those of us who live here in Ugly Creek. We have a moral obligation to rid ourselves of this kind of problem, so let's do what should have been done long ago. Let's zone our beloved community to prevent small businesses from blighting our neighborhoods. Thank you."

She turned and walked back to her seat, shooting a smirk in Ace's direction. Vanetti was right behind her, but as he turned to the microphone, Mayor Paradise spoke. "Hold on a minute there. I think Mr. Ellison should have a chance to speak."

Vanetti shot an angry glance toward the mayor, but he returned to his seat.

I gave Ace's hand a squeeze, and he smiled weakly before he stood.

He walked to the mike with his shoulders back, chin up, determination etched on his face. "Hello," he said. "I'm Ace Ellison, and I take care of unwanted animals. I understand the reasoning for not wanting a rescue operation in a residential area, but there are good reasons why I run things the way I do. First, I actually live onsite. If there are problems, I can deal with them immediately. On the other hand, most of the problems I deal with are simple misunderstandings about what I do and why I do it. Second, animals need an environment where they can run and be animals. I personally deal almost exclusively with dogs, and some of them are large. These animals need a big space in which to run and play. Having that space prevents the temptation to escape in order to run. My yard is large and securely fenced. It's also far enough from the forest to make it unlikely wild animals will injure mine. Third, volunteers. Most of the volunteers who help me with the dogs are teenagers. Being near home makes it easier for them. By the way, the volunteer work gets these kids away from video games, shows them the value of physical labor, teaches compassion, and looks great on a college application."

He took a moment to shift the note cards in his hand. "I chose a house whose yard opened to the woods. I live at the end of a road, and pretty far away from any neighbor. I have spoken to the other people who live on my road, and none of them have any problem with me, and my dogs, living there. I have a building behind my house where most of the rescues live. That building is kept clean, the animals are fed, watered, bathed, and walked at least twice daily. New dogs are separated from the rest until a vet is satisfied they are healthy." He looked down a moment, then back at the city council.

"I love animals. I focus on dogs, but I wouldn't hesitate to help a cat or cow or donkey. We as humans share this earth with a huge variety of other creatures, but we tend to ignore them most of the time, the worst being our pets. We've bred these animals over thousands of years to serve our purposes. Over time they have lost many of the survival instincts they once had, and are now under-equipped to survive without human care. We brought them into our homes. Many people love and care for their pets, but there are those who can't, or won't. That's where people like me come in. We take the animals, in my case dogs, and care for them until another home can be found. The alternative is killing the animals. Yes, there are no-kill shelters. They tend to be overwhelmed and many depend on people like me to take some of the animals off their hands. I love what I do, but I wish there wasn't a need. I'd be very happy to close my rescue and just be a photographer, but as long as there are animals who need me, I'll do my best to help them. Thank you for hearing me out."

He turned and walked back to sit beside me.

The room was quiet. Totally quiet, as if the entire audience was holding its collective breath.

And then Terri stood. "I'd like to speak if I could. Not about the animal shelter, but about the zoning itself and other consequences of the change."

"Go ahead," the mayor said.

Terri went to the microphone. "My name is Terri Quinn, and I'm a novelist. What you may not realize is that people like me, writers, artists, crafters, are legally small business owners. If this zoning ordinance is passed, Ace Ellison will not be the only person affected. Artistic types don't normally need a storefront or an office other than a workspace in his or her home, but this law would force us to use one anyway. For some the cost would force them to give up something they love. For others, like me, it would be a major inconvenience. Do you really want to send the message that Ugly Creek is intolerant of writers, artists, and even people like Miss Sunflower?" She shot a grin at the tall redhead. "I'm sure most of you have one of her quilts on your bed, or one of her gorgeous hand-knitted sweaters in your closet. She is legally a small business owner. Please consider the impact of rezoning carefully before you make a decision. Thank you for allowing me to speak."

She sat down as the sound of protest came from the Carlisle section of the room. She's a friend of Ace's, girlfriend's cousin, owns a dog…

The gavel came down and the mayor's voice sounded through the uproar. "Quiet!"

As the noise receded, I saw the council members conferring. After a moment, the mayor looked into the audience. "It seems we are ready for a vote."

I grabbed Ace's hand and he clung to mine as each council member in turn voted no to the change, his grip lessening with each vote. By the time they were finished, I could feel him trembling. I glanced at him and saw tears in his eyes. I reached over with my free hand and squeezed his shoulder. He covered my hand with his free one and pressed mine against him.

Meanwhile, on the other side of the room, the anti-Ace people expressed their disagreement with the vote.

The mayor was once again trying to restore order—and failing.

Her face was purple as she stood and yelled, "Anybody who doesn't want to spend the night in jail had better sit down and shut up!"

When quiet again descended, she looked out into the gathering. "Before we met here tonight, my fellow council members and I studied the current zoning ordinances, the laws regarding them, and the few changes to them over the years. We also looked at the ordinances of several other small towns. What we discovered was that in this, like so many other things, Ugly Creek is proudly different. Our zoning ordinances are nothing like those of other towns. Ours are basic divisions to allow for downtown businesses, residential areas, and to protect our beloved forest. Other than that, we try to work through problems as a community."

Ace tightened his grip on my hand again. I rubbed his shoulder and tried to give him my strength.

"We're a special little place here," the mayor continued, "and I don't think anyone wants to see that change. We believe that those who feel drawn here most likely belong." She glanced toward Terri. "We certainly don't want to discourage writers, artists, or makers of beautiful quilts." A gentle laugh rippled through the audience. "Or people doing good things for our furry friends." She smiled at Ace. "Thank you for your hard work." She slammed the gavel down. "Meeting adjourned."

The room went wild. But I was too busy hugging Ace to care. He held me tight until Jake said, "The rest of us would like to congratulate him too."

I squeezed him firmly before I let him go.

He met my gaze and held it for a moment.

"Thank you," he whispered. Then he turned to accept congratulations from the happy group surrounding him.

Across the way, grumbling conversation became more heated by the minute. Terri and I glanced at each other before we moved simultaneously to stand between the dissenters and Ace. Seconds later, others joined us. As the group of us moved toward the door, Ace was surrounded by a small army of amateur bodyguards.

I caught a glimpse of Miz Carlisle, who looked like she could bite the head off a chicken. Then she glared at me, and I looked down to make sure I wasn't growing feathers. On boy, living next to her would not be fun.

I looked away, only to see Lily glaring, but not at Ace. The person she shot hatred toward was Steve Zapata. The woman was seriously weird. But that was irrelevant. All that mattered was that the man I loved wasn't being forced to leave the place he'd made a home.

Then we were through the door and outside. The group walked together to the entrance to the gravel parking area. There we were met by Ace's SUV and one of his teenage volunteers.

Ace chuckled. "So that's why you wanted my keys, Keith."

"Let's all go have dinner and celebrate," Jake said.

Ace sighed. "Sounds good, but I think I've had enough excitement for one day. Could we have a rain check?"

"Of course." Jake clapped a hand on Ace's shoulder. "Go home and get some rest."

He glanced at me and winked.

"Or whatever."

Ace, apparently oblivious to his friend's implication, looked around at the surrounding supporters. "Thank you, all of you. I can't believe how great you've all been. I'm a lucky man to have such great friends." He wiped at his eyes. "I'd better go before I embarrass myself."

There was a round of hand-shaking, back-slapping, and a lot of hugging. Finally there was only Ace, Terri, and me.

She hugged him and turned to go, but I caught her arm. "Be careful. She's not going to be happy."

"I know. You be careful too."

She gave each of us the most serious look I'd ever seen on her. She hugged me and squeezed Ace's arm, then headed to her Fiat.

Ace turned to me.

"I'm so glad that's over."

"Are you okay?"

"I will be."

His hands settled on my shoulders. "Would you come home with me? I think we have some things to discuss." He swallowed. "And honestly, I don't want to be alone right now."

"Of course I will." In spite of the ripple of worry the talk word shot through me, I wanted to be with him.

"Want to ride with me?"

"Thanks, but I have my car. If you want, I could pick up some dinner on the way."

"Sounds good."

We got in our respective vehicles and headed out.

Chapter 20

By the time I arrived at Ace's house it was dark, but the light on his porch welcomed me. I grabbed the bag of tacos and walked toward the house. I was halfway across the lawn when the door opened and Dusty came running out, followed closely by Ace.

I scooped Dusty up, laughing as she wiggled and licked my face. By the time Ace reached us, Dusty was done greeting me and struggling hard to get to the tacos.

"I think I'm jealous," he said.

I shifted the wiggling ball of fur again. "Don't worry; I'm sure she'll play with you later."

He growled and pulled me into his arms. His greedy lips covered mine as if he were starving for me. Hell, he might be, I was certainly hungry for him. Then the furball decided she was being neglected and began wiggling and digging in her claws in an effort to climb up to our faces.

Ace backed up, keeping one hand on the dog and one on me.

"Let's go inside."

He took the tacos and Dusty tried hard to change humans. "Traitor," I told her.

She gave me an innocent look before she went back to struggling to get to the bag of food.

In the house, Ace put the bag on the table, and I put

Dusty on the floor. She ran a couple of laps around the room, then sat staring at the table.

"You know you can't have any," Ace told her. She lay down with her chin on her paws and managed to look both adorable and pathetic.

Ace put plates and colas on the table and I unloaded the tacos. We sat down and dove in. Seems both of us were hungrier than we'd thought.

When we came up for air, I reached over to touch Ace's hand. "I'm really glad you can stay. You love this town." I studied my food for a moment. "I kinda do too."

Ace chuckled. "Even with your crazy neighbor, everybody's psychic aunt, and Bigfoot?"

"Not to mention the unicorn." As soon as the words were out of my mouth, the pieces slid together. For a moment I just sat there and thought about how many ways I could be wrong.

"Are you okay, honey?"

"I need to talk to Steve. Now."

He didn't hesitate. "Let's go."

As he drove, Ace called ahead. Fifteen minutes later we pulled into a long driveway leading up to a beautiful brick, large yet modest home.

Steve opened the door and I winced when I saw the worry and fatigue that lined his face. "I'm sorry to bother you. I know you have to be exhausted but I think this is something you need to know."

"Come in."

He waved us into the den,

Liza came in behind us, carrying a tray with cookies and colas. "If you prefer something else I can get it for you."

"Relax, both of you. I just want to tell you what I know, because I think it might be important."

Steve lowered himself into a chair. "Okay, what's up?"

Liza perched on the arm of her husband's chair, and all eyes were on me.

I swallowed and dove in head first. "Steve, how well do you know Lily Bennett?"

He frowned. "Lily who?"

In a sweet, intimate movement, Liza ran her fingers through her husband's hair. "Lily Roth, she married Ken Bennett."

He nodded. "Oh yeah, I went to school with her. I haven't seen her in years."

"She was at the zoning meeting," I told him. "And she gave you one of those looks where you're lucky to be alive."

He shrugged. "I have no idea why she would do that."

"I think I might." Liza shifted her perch on the arm of his chair. "Lily has had it bad for Steve since high school."

He frowned up at her. "I didn't know that."

Liza smiled down at him, her hand still tangled in his hair. "No need for you to know."

Steve grinned. "Keeping me all for yourself, huh?"

"Hell yes. Nobody's getting their grubby hands on my guy."

She leaned down and their lips met in a kiss that had me looking away.

Ace cleared his throat. "Should we come back later?"

It was another long few seconds before the two

separated. Steve looked toward us, his smile one of smug satisfaction.

"What were we talking about?"

"Lily," I reminded him. "I saw her with one of your security guys. His name was Ronnie."

He frowned. "And?"

"He was talking about leaving tonight, but she said she needed more time to get ready. Then he said something about getting caught. I assumed they were talking about the affair but later I started to wonder about that. He actually said something about going to jail." I swallowed in an effort to clear my dry throat. "Then Lily gave you the mother of all glares."

Steve's eyes widened. "You're sure the man's name was Ronnie?"

I nodded. "That's what she called him. This guy is medium height, brown hair, he wore a Vols ball cap."

Steve sat for a moment as he chewed on his bottom lip. Without warning, he rose from his chair, grabbed his phone from a side table, and punched in some numbers. "I have some information I think you'll want to hear."

He paced the room as he passed on what I had overheard. I held my breath—literally—as I waited for him to finish.

"Breathe," Ace whispered, poking me with his elbow.

I realized the world was getting fuzzy and sucked in breath. "Thanks," I whispered, and he winked.

Before I could shove that adorable image out of my mind, Steve clicked his phone off and came back into the room. "I talked to the head agent on the case, Special Agent Anderson, and he was very interested."

Steve sighed. "To be honest, there have been questions about Ronnie, but nothing concrete. He's going to look into what you told me, and call me if he learns anything important. I'll let you know what he says."

Ace wrapped an arm around me. "Let's go so they can get some rest."

I knew Ace was right. Steve and Liza looked totally worn out but it took resolve to stand, hug them both, and allow Ace to escort me to his car.

"This feels kind of anticlimactic," I said.

He grinned at me from the driver's seat. "If you're feeling anticlimactic, I think I can help you with that."

I didn't know whether to laugh, roll my eyes, or tell him to pull off the road so that we could get started. "You're something else."

"Well, if you aren't interested…"

"I didn't say that."

He grinned as he took my hand in his, and for the rest of the trip attraction tingled between us.

We barely got in the house before we had our hands all over each other. We stumbled up the stairs, almost making it inside the bedroom before clothes started flying. Then we flew too, again and again.

When we finally came back down to earth, I lay warm and happy against the man I love as I told myself he wouldn't have shared what he had with me if he planned on walking out of my life. Still, when I remembered the serious expression on his face when he said we needed to talk, something inside me whimpered in fear.

I wrapped my arm over his chest and snuggled against him. I couldn't imagine the rest of my life without Ace in it.

Chapter 21

The next morning Ace was up and showered before I managed to pull my exhausted self out of bed. "You wore me out," I told him.

He just grinned. "Take your time. I'll go deal with the dogs then we can have breakfast."

He gave me a quick kiss before he headed out.

As I showered and dressed, I tried to convince myself he hadn't seemed distant this morning. He was just tired, that's all.

The mouthwatering smell of bacon, eggs, toast, and coffee drew me down the stairs. "You weren't kidding about breakfast, I see."

He glanced my way from where he stood in front of the stove, spatula in hand.

"I wouldn't kid about something like that."

I got myself some coffee. "What can I do to help?"

"Nothing."

He gave me a quick kiss then sat me down at the table. "Relax. I'm cooking."

"I could get used to this." I saw how he froze for a second, and decided to change the subject. "I called Terri to let her know I'm okay. When she found out you hadn't kidnapped me and swept me away to some exotic place, she was disappointed. I'm not sure if it's because she's a romantic, or because she wants to get rid of me."

"Maybe a little bit of both?"

"Probably."

He put food on the table and sat next to me. I scooped up a bite, and the buttery goodness of perfectly cooked scrambled eggs made my tongue very happy. "This is delicious," I told him.

"Thank you."

We were mostly quiet while we ate, except for a bit of good-natured teasing. I began to believe everything was fine. Maybe my fear had gotten the best of me, and I'd imagined things that were never there. By the time we finished the meal, I was relaxed and feeling good about being with this amazing man.

"I'd like to talk, if that's okay with you."

"Sure." And my relaxed got up and ran out the door.

He shifted in his seat, looking around as if gathering information, or strength. I swallowed so hard it hurt my throat.

"I've moved a lot over the past few years. Most people aren't as accepting of me and my rescue as they are here in Ugly Creek."

"This is a very accepting place."

He nodded while swiping his thumb and forefinger over his eyes. "I was freaking amazed at what happened yesterday."

I touched his arm. "A lot of people care about you."

He looked at me as he smiled. "And I plan to thank God every single day for that." He looked away again, and his frown returned. "As I was saying, most places aren't so accepting. You're right about my loving this town, especially now that I see how great the people really are and how many friends I have here." He took a hard, deep breath. "For a while there I was sure I'd have to leave. I was convinced I would have to keep moving and maybe never find a place where I really belong."

He looked at me then with those beautiful green eyes.

"I couldn't ask another person to make that sacrifice with me. Even if I love her more than I've ever loved anyone in my whole life."

Stunned into silence, I could do nothing but stare into those gorgeous eyes. My cell sounded a message alert, but I didn't care. All that mattered was the man in front of me.

Ace's phone chirped from across the room but he too ignored the sound. Then mine sounded again, and I pulled the damn cell out of my pocket so I could throw it out the window. When it sounded again I automatically swiped my finger across the screen. Then I saw the text and my breath sucked in. It was from Terri. "Home. Nine-one-one." I moved it so Ace could see, just as his phone sounded again.

"Let's go."

He started to stand up, but I grabbed his arm. "I love you too."

There was a second of connection between us before my cell sounded again. Then we ran.

****

When we arrived at the house, Miz Carlisle stood on my porch, screaming. Vanetti stood near her with a rope in his hand.

As soon as the Xterra stopped, we bailed out on either side. Ace was right beside me as I rushed up the steps.

"What the hell is going on?"

Our neighbor glared hard at me. "That mangy mutt of your cousin's attacked my sweet Bumpkins. He's at the veterinarian's right now."

I glared right back. "Trixie didn't hurt him."

"How would you know? You weren't even here." Her glare jumped from me to Ace and back.

"I know Trixie," I told her.

"I agree," Ace said. "Trixie wouldn't attack a smaller animal."

My cell sounded and I pulled it out of my pocket. The text was from Terri. "A bobcat attacked Bumpkins. Trixie saved the cat's life."

I showed the text to Ace, and he nodded. "Makes sense."

The sound of a car stopping had me looking over my shoulder.

Ken Bennett slid out of his cruiser and came toward us. I was relieved to see a friend, but seeing him reminded me of Lily with another man. I so wanted to punch that idiot woman.

"I'm glad you're here, officer," Vanetti said. "There is a vicious dog in that house, and I mean to take it to the pound."

Ken raised an eyebrow. "When was it you became dog catcher?"

"It's my understanding that private citizens are allowed to do their part to help police our wonderful little town."

Ken shook his head. "If this animal is as dangerous as you're claiming, a professional should handle the capture and containment. If I stood back and allowed you to do this I would be remiss in my duties."

Vanetti's face went red. "I have assisted my cousins many times when they grabbed dangerous dogs. I can handle this as well as anybody."

"I'm sorry, sir. I can't allow you to do something that might cause you harm."

Miz Carlisle took a step toward Ken. "How about my Bumpkins? Nobody protected him from that horrible animal!"

Ken took his notebook out of his pocket. "Did you see this attack, ma'am?"

"Yes."

"No!" Terri shouted from inside the house.

Miz Carlisle's nostrils flared. "What else could have hurt my baby?"

"We live next to woods," Ace pointed out. "There are a lot of animals out there capable of hurting a housecat."

"You're telling me some kind of wild animal came out of the woods, when the most likely culprit is that mangy beast holed up in your house?"

"Trixie didn't hurt your cat," I told her, knowing I was wasting my breath.

Ken pulled his phone from a pocket, frowning when he looked at it. "I have to take this," he said as he took a few steps away from the porch.

"That beast has been after my sweet baby ever since you moved into Ruth's house. Believe me, she will hear all about this when she gets back."

Ken, his face drained of almost all its color, returned. "Look, there's nothing I can do until I get the report from the vet." He pointed at Vanetti. "You go home. Miz Carlisle, you too."

"That dog hurt my baby."

"There is nothing I can do until we get the medical report."

"I can take that mutt to the pound where it can't hurt anybody."

"Go home, Vanetti. I don't have time to deal with you right now." He looked at us. "Keep the dog in the house until this is straightened out."

"We will," I said.

"You'd better." Vanetti puffed like a steam engine trying to climb K2.

Ken spun around. "Go home, Vanetti. You need to stay the hell out of things that don't concern you."

The man opened his mouth, but when Ken stepped toward him, he turned and stomped toward his house.

Miz Carlisle gave me an eat-dirt-and-die glare, then headed home.

"Keep Trixie inside and try to hold things together." He lowered his voice. "Lily's in FBI custody. I have to go." He rushed to his cruiser then pulled out and tore down the road.

Ace's hand settled on my shoulder.

"It's not your fault."

Maybe not, but it sure as hell felt like it was.

Chapter 22

"Trixie would never hurt another animal. How can anybody even think that?" Terri pranced around the living room like an over-stimulated puppy, and she'd been doing it for a good hour. Who needs television?

"We know. Ken knows. Everybody knows except Crazy Woman and Hateful Man." I was wasting my breath, but I really should try to calm her down. Right?

Ace laughed quietly. "Crazy Woman and Hateful Man. Sounds like a superhero cartoon."

"Most people don't know Trixie. They don't what a good dog she is." Terri looked at me. "You need to walk her so people can meet her. It's not like I can do it myself. Well I can, but some idiot like Vanetti would probably grab her and put her in the pound." She shivered, looking for all the world like a dog shaking water off her fur.

Ace chuckled. "How could I not have seen it sooner? It's so obvious now." His cell buzzed. He swiped and sat it on the coffee table. "Hey Ken, you're on speakerphone."

"The official report from the vet says the cat's going to be fine. And that the injury was caused by a large feline."

"See," Terri said, "I told you."

"I called Miz Carlisle, the vet even talked to her, but she's convinced there's a conspiracy and we're all in on it."*

"She's nuts," Terri said.

"You might be right, Terri." The sound of a deep breath came through the phone. "I'd come back out there, but I really need to be with Lily right now."

"Take care of your family," Ace told him. "We'll deal with the crazies."

"Thanks. Let me know if anything happens."

Ace looked from me to Terri and back again.

"We're on our own, ladies."

"I'm starving," Terri said. "What do you want to do for lunch?"

"How about we order pizza?" I was really not in the mood to cook. "Terri can pay."

"You're just jealous because Trixie's fur is so soft and shiny."

I rolled my eyes. "Yes, I'm jealous of you because of your alter ego's nice fur."

"See, you admit it." As she turned, I saw the smile she was trying to hide.

"I'll call in the order. Ace, meat or veggie toppings?"

"Both."

She rolled her eyes dramatically. "Humans!"

He didn't miss a beat. "Dogs!"

She snorted as she turned to get her phone.

"I should call and make sure my dogs get taken care of."

He kissed me quickly then pulled out his phone.

I smiled as I looked back and forth between them. They acted like brother and sister. That thought brought another, and I shoved it out of my head. No way would I let myself consider marriage and family. I'd been caregiver all my life; I didn't need to tie myself down to that kind of situation again.

Something about that thought seemed wrong, but I refused to consider what that might be.

****

"Brave of you to risk your life to save your mortal enemy."

Terri looked at me as she grabbed the last slice of pizza.

"Bumpkins may be the spawn of Satan, but he doesn't deserve to be eaten by a bobcat."

For a moment, I was afraid Ace was choking, but then he started to laugh.

"Who would have thought the words 'Bumpkins' and 'spawn of Satan' would be used in the same sentence? And it even makes sense."

Terri grinned. "'Tis a strange family you have chosen to align yourself with."

"I'm a strange fellow. I should fit right in."

I leaned back and watched the teasing play until they started clearing the table. "I can do that."

"No." They looked at each other and laughed at their shared rejection of my offer.

Why I was stung by the opportunity to relax was beyond me, but I was. "Fine."

Ace turned to look at me. "Why can't you just let somebody else handle things for a while?"

"Because she's a control freak."

Terri winked at me.

"But we love her anyway."

Ace gave me a big sexy smile then grabbed the garbage to take out.

A few minutes later, the kitchen was spotless and

the three of us were back in the living room. Conversation was minimal but I was fine with sitting quietly on the couch next to Ace. He held my hand in his, and I felt more relaxed than I had in a long time.

Terri wiggled in her seat, but that wasn't abnormal for her. The girl was human, but her canine side was always just under the surface.

She shot to her feet, startling a yelp from me.

"I don't think I can stay cooped up in here all night. Trixie needs to run."

"She can run through the house," Ace suggested.

"It's not the same." She paced for a while, then stopped and looked at us. "I could drive somewhere, far enough away nobody would know, and Trixie could run in the woods."

"No."

She glared at me so hard I thought her eyes might pop out.

"You are not my mother, Shay. You really need to stop acting like you are." With that she turned and marched into her bedroom.

I stared until I realized my mouth was hanging open. I closed it as I realized Ace watched me. "I don't act like her mother."

Ace's raised eyebrow told me what I seriously did not want to hear.

"She's so irresponsible."

He looked away for a moment, then met my gaze.

"She seems pretty responsible to me. She's kept her secret all her life. She couldn't have done that if she wasn't responsible."

Realization hit me hard. I'd come to Ugly Creek determined to enjoy not having to take care of anyone

237

but myself. Instead, I'd spent the whole time looking for people to take care of. I groaned and leaned my head back against the couch.

"You don't have to take care of everybody."

He cupped his hand under my chin and tipped it up.

"You could let somebody take care of you."

His lips gently touched mine.

"You know what I think?" he murmured against my mouth, "I think you're afraid if we don't need you, we won't love you."

He looked deep into my eyes.

"You're wrong."

Before I could stop myself, my greatest fear popped out, "Mom could relapse."

He gently brushed a lock of hair off my face.

"If she does, we'll make sure she gets the help she needs."

"*We?*" The thought was incredulous.

"I want you in my life, Shay. If that's okay with you."

"I'm scared. Wow, I can't believe I just admitted that to you."

He kissed me softly then whispered against my mouth. "Don't be scared, sweetheart. I'd never hurt you, and I'll kill anybody else who tries."

He tugged me against him.

"You aren't alone anymore."

I leaned against his warm strong body, enjoying the feel of loving arms around me. Tears stung my eyes as I realized how much I'd needed this feeling, how long it had been since I'd felt it, how grateful I was to Ace for giving me such a wonderful gift.

A high-pitched scream shattered the quiet.

Chapter 23

I leapt to my feet and rushed toward the door just behind Ace. Terri tore from her bedroom, all of us reaching the porch together then sprinting down the steps and across the yard. Movement toward the back caught my attention, and I saw a streak of orange and black fur leap over Miz Carlisle's back fence and head into the woods.

Miz Carlisle stood on her side of the fence, her face pale and her hand on her chest, which heaved in an effort to take in air.

Ace got to her first and actually had his hand on her shoulder. "Are you all right?" he asked.

"I thought it was a dog." The woman's voice shook. "But it was some kind of wild animal."

"Bobcat," Terri said.

"How do you know?" The words were more an honest question and not so much the sour attitude Miz Carlisle always seemed to have.

"I saw it heading back to the woods," Terri replied. "It was the same cat that attacked Bumpkins earlier."

"It really wasn't your dog that attacked my baby."

Terri walked over to our neighbor.

"Look, I know Trixie and Bumpkins don't get along very well, but I can't imagine either of them seriously hurting the other." She shrugged. "In fact, I think their conflict is more playful than real."

A glance at my cousin attested to the sincerity in her voice. Well, this was an interesting turn of events.

"Maybe not," Miz C said. "But I still don't trust that mutt."

"I understand." Terri said. "Trixie doesn't trust Bumpkins either."

I glanced toward the back where the bobcat had made its hasty exit. That cat had hurt Bumpkins and just a while ago it had come close enough to Miz C to scare her pretty badly. If it hadn't been for her scream and our rush into the yard, who knows what it would have done. "We need to report the bobcat to wildlife control."

"I agree," Ace said. "I'll be happy to call, but I think we should all go inside until this is dealt with."

"Excellent idea." Miz C glanced furtively toward the back then turned her gaze on her house. In spite of her words, it wasn't hard to see the worry in her eyes.

Ace jumped the fence and offered the woman his arm. "Allow me to escort you to your door."

She hooked her hand through his elbow and he led her toward her house. At one point I heard what sounded suspiciously like a female giggle. I shook my head in an effort to kick myself back into reality.

"Brave man, that Ace."

"He's a nice guy." Pride rose in my chest as I spoke. I watched him as he headed back our way.

He leaped the fence, then grabbed an arm of each of us.

"I was serious about going inside. We know nothing about this bobcat, except it's vicious."

Terri jerked her arm away from his hold. "He's not vicious! He wants to play but he doesn't realize how big and strong he is."

I searched her expression and decided she was serious. "So, this huge wild animal likes to play with housecats?"

Somehow Terri had slid behind Ace and me, and was nudging us firmly toward the front door. Ah, collies are herding animals. She was herding us. I bit back the laugh.

"He's just a kitten," she said, as she pushed us through the front door.

"So the bobcat's a kitten, and you and Satan's spawn are buddies."

Ace frowned in her direction. "I wanted to talk to you about that. I'm pretty sure Hugh doesn't share your new affection for Bumpkins."

Terri looked at the floor. "I don't think Bumpkins meant to hurt Hugh. He's used to Trixie and she knows when to duck."

I let out a big sigh. "I think maybe Bumpkins getting hurt upset you more than you want to admit."

Her lips tightened and she turned away but not before I caught the glisten of tears in her eyes.

"I was so scared. Blood was everywhere and he was making this little crying sound."

She wiped at her eyes. "I couldn't even stay with him. I barked to get help, and Miz C ran out screaming at me, and I had to get away before she hurt me."

I wrapped my arms around her as she cried. My heart bled at the thought of how horrible that had to be.

Ace stood between the kitchen and living room, his phone in his hand, and concern in his eyes. "The vet had already notified wildlife control about the attack. Of course, he didn't know what species did the attacking."

Terri had straightened up and wiped her eyes. "Did you tell them it was a bobcat?"

Ace nodded. "I told them you witnessed the attack out your window and we saw enough to confirm what you said."

"All I saw was a brownish-orange and black streak," I said, "but it was the right size and shape. I suppose Miz Carlisle got the best look at the critter."

Terri rolled her eyes. "God only knows what she'll say."

Ace put a hand on Terri's shoulder. "Unlike our local dog pound jerks, the wildlife people are exceptional. They'll find the cat in no time."

"I hope they don't hurt him."

"They won't. I made a point of telling them he ran from Miz Carlisle."

A car pulled up outside, and I went to the window. A rough-looking pickup was parked on the side of the road in front of our house.

"That didn't take him long."

Ace looked at me.

"I asked Keith to bring Hugh over here. Hugh hates being in the kennel, but if I let him in the house alone he'd destroy it. I hope you don't mind."

"Awesome!" Terri all but squealed.

"You can't play outside," Ace reminded her.

"Or destroy Aunt Ruth's house," I added.

"Oh great Mom *and* Dad." She bounded off to a window to watch for her playmate.

"Come out with me, and you can bring in Dusty."

"Dusty?"

He gave me a little smile as he shrugged. "She

wanted to see you."

I laughed. "So you're psychically connected with a dog now?"

He wrapped an arm around me as we headed to Keith's truck.

"You don't have to read minds to know she's crazy about you."

"I sort of like her too."

We got Hugh and Dusty from Keith. He pulled out and we had started toward the house, when a brown BMW pulled in where the truck had been.

"Get Dusty in the house, I'll be there in a minute."

"Hurry up." I glanced around, but saw no sign of any animals, wild or otherwise. Yes, Terri had said the animal wasn't dangerous, but I didn't want to take any chances. Dusty wiggled, and I was glad to be at the porch. If the dog jumped out of my arms it'd be hard to catch her.

As I opened the door, I caught a glimpse of Ace hustling Steve and Hugh across the lawn. They were seconds behind me entering the living room, where Trixie met her friend. The big dogs took off through Aunt Ruth's house, and Dusty tore off after them.

"Steve, would you like some sweet tea?"

"I'd love some."

"Ace?"

"I'll help you." Ace stood.

"I can help too."

"No" I said. "You're exhausted, just sit there and relax. It'll only take us a minute."

Steve sat back, relief obvious in his features.

It only took a couple of minutes to get the tea and some store-bought cookies.

"No homemade?" Ace's disappointment almost made him look like a little kid. Except for that sexy all male body, of course.

"I'll make some tomorrow."

"Thanks, gorgeous."

He kissed me and we took the drinks and cookies back into the living room.

Steve took a healthy sip of the tea before he asked, "So there's a bobcat loose around here?"

"There is," Ace told him. "It attacked the housecat next door."

"Scary."

"Woof!"

I turned to see Trixie giving me the collie version of her glare. Not nearly as effective, in my opinion, as the human kind. "Terri saw the attack out the window, and she said it looked more like the bobcat was just trying to play."

"Sounds plausible," Steve said. "Still scary, though."

"How're you and Liza doing?"

"Better, now that it looks like this crap might be over soon. By the way, Liza said to tell you that she would have come, but she's on a video chat with her best friend. She and Madison haven't had a lot of time to talk lately."

The name sounded familiar. "The serious journalist?"

Steve chuckled. "Not so much since she hooked up with Mac and took off to make documentaries."

"I wasn't sure if she and that McFain guy were going to kill each other or admit they were crazy in love."

That name was familiar. "McFain? The guy who screwed up that senator's life?"

"That's the one," Steve said.

"He seems like an okay guy," Ace said.

"I always felt bad for him," I said. "He just discovered the cover-up; he didn't cause it." I turned my gaze on Steve. "Unfortunately, I don't think you came here just to chit-chat."

He smiled. "I wish. After all this break-in stuff is over, I would like nothing better than to get together to chit-chat and enjoy the company of friends."

"I'll grill the steaks," Ace said.

"Sounds great." Steve's expression grew serious as he turned to me and leaned forward in his seat.

"I actually came to thank you, Shay. You were right about Ronnie Wilkins. He was the perpetrator of the break-in and theft. Ronnie swears he would never have sold the materials or data to anybody and what they've found so far backs him up. He took the stuff then put it in a safe deposit box. He's trying to take all the blame, and refuses to implicate Lily. She, on the other hand, all but fell over herself blaming him. The feds will be sorting it out for a while, but apparently there is plenty of evidence that implicates both of them."

"Poor Ken." My heart ached for the nice man.

Steve nodded. "I feel really bad for him, but I'm glad this crazy thing is almost over."

"I'm glad I could help. Even if I did manage to hurt another friend in the process."

"It's not your fault, honey."

Ace took my hand in his and squeezed gently.

"Gotta agree with your guy there. Lily got herself

in trouble because of some stupid, decade-old high school crush on me. Who does that? Somehow I think Ken will be better off without her."

"She seemed so nice," I said.

"So did Ted Bundy," Steve pointed out.

I nodded. "True, along with Phillip Markoff, Albert Fish, Jeffery Dahmer, Dorthea Puente, and quite a few others." I realized the men were staring at me, so I smiled innocently.

"How does a sweet woman like you know all those names? Right off the top of your head, no less."

It was hard to hold back my amusement at Steve's wide-eyed expression.

Ace laughed. "That's my Shay. You never know what to expect."

Those words might have irritated me, except for the warm, caring look in his eyes and the way he'd said, "My Shay." Like his to love and care for. So I smiled like the smitten woman I was.

Steve's laughter caught our attention.

"So the mighty Ace has fallen under a woman's spell. Congratulations."

He grinned at me.

"Condolences to the lady."

"Asswipe," Ace muttered.

Steve just laughed again as he stood. "I'd better get back home. There's still a gazillion things to do to get the business back in operation."

"Gazillion? Technical term?" I teased.

"Yep."

I laughed as I hugged him, and he walked out with Ace, the two of them quickly sliding into a testosterone-fueled insult-fest. I smiled as I watched them walk toward Steve's car. Men complain that we're complicated, but they're just as complicated and difficult to understand as women. Except for when they're insulting each other like little boys.

My thoughts slipped from the show outside, and I considered what would happen now. Guilt still welled up in me with the slightest provocation, but the relief I saw on Steve's face made me feel better. I'd done what I had to do. I couldn't hold myself responsible for the bad choices of two people I barely knew.

"Steve looks much better."

I squealed, which had Terri shaking with laughter. I glared. "Nice how you get amusement from startling your cousin."

"Sorry."

She didn't look at all sorry. On the other hand, "At least you're dressed."

She rolled her eyes. "Hugh doesn't want to see me naked."

The door opened and Ace walked in as he said "Thank you" into his cell before turning it off. "A friend of mine in wildlife management just called. They found the cat, and about an hour later they also discovered his mother and sister. The mom has an injured leg, but they don't think it's serious. Just enough for the little guy to get away from her and create havoc. They're going to fix her up and make sure there's nothing else to be concerned about. When they're all three cleared, they'll be released into the wild somewhere where humans won't bother them."

I let out a breath and leaned into Ace's waiting arms. "Thank God."

Terri did a little jumping dance. "I'm so glad the

little kitty is all right. And his mommy and sister."

She danced toward the kitchen, and I turned back to Ace. He glanced toward the dancing shapeshifter. "Never a boring moment around here."

There was the sound of the doggie door. Twice.

"That's for sure."

Just then, Dusty leaped off the couch and shot like a rocket toward the kitchen. A moment later, we heard the sound of the doggie door a third time.

"Good."

Ace pulled me against him.

"I hate boring."

His lips captured mine and heat rushed through me. For a moment all I could do was enjoy the feeling, then I pushed back enough to say, "You know she can see and smell things we can't. There is no privacy around her."

"Maybe she'll just have to get used to us," he whispered against my lips before he recaptured them.

****

Sometime during the night, Dusty woke me up whining. I found her standing beside the bed, looking up at me with the cutest little face I'd ever seen. I couldn't just ignore her, so I picked her up and put her on my chest. She licked my face, and I laughed quietly.

"Keep spoiling her like that, and I'll never find a forever home for her."

My breath caught at the idea of Dusty giving sweet lick-kisses to somebody else. "Don't even think about it."

Ace scratched the top of Dusty's soft little head. She immediately hopped off my chest and wiggled her way into the almost nonexistent space between Ace and me.

"I think maybe she's already found a new home," he said.

"You might be right." I told him then looked at Dusty. "But you and I need to have a talk about your preferred sleeping spot."

She raised her head and looked at me with big, innocent brown eyes, then turned to snuggle back into the warmth between the human bodies.

"I'm thinking crates for each of our bedrooms might be in order."

I narrowed my eyes at him, but he just chuckled.

"I love her too, but there are times when I don't want anything between us." He ran the tip of his index finger over one breast, making a point to linger at the nipple.

I gasped.

"Absolutely nothing between us," he whispered.

Dusty had to go back to the floor for a while, and she whined about it. I felt bad for her, until Ace made me forget everything but what I was feeling.

****

Ace left early to check on his dogs, and Terri was hard at work on her next masterpiece. I sat at the kitchen table, computer in front of me, Dusty on my lap, and my fingers slowly typing their way through one of the last scenes of my contracted book. Almost there, and then I would be free to work on my romantic suspense. My agent was interested in the two chapters and rough synopsis I'd thrown together and sent her right after I'd called to admit I wanted to change my subgenre, although we agreed it would be best to wait until the manuscript was finished before she approached any editor about it. The important thing was she hadn't freaked out about my desire to take my writing career in a different direction.

"Bumpkins is home!"

I put Dusty on the floor and we headed to the living room where Terri performed another little bouncy dance.

"Will you go over there with me?"

"Sure." I leaned down to pet my furry sidekick's head. "You stay in the house. I'll be right back."

I stood and started toward the front, not totally surprised that Trixie had taken Terri's place. I opened the door, glanced back toward the unhappy puppy staring at me. "Be right back." I headed out with Trixie right beside me.

Ms. Carlisle carried Bumpkins, wrapped in a blanket like a human baby, in her arms

I got as close to the fence as I could so I could see better. "How is he?"

She cast a suspicious look toward Trixie before she answered me. "He's doing much better, aren't you, my little sweetie?" She made kissy noises toward the cat, who graced her with a moment of consideration before turning his gaze back to Trixie.

"Would you hold him down a bit so she can see he's all right?"

She looked at me like I'd suggested feeding Bumpkins to Trixie. It took a couple of tense minutes for her to think about it, but she gave a surrendering nod and leaned down so Trixie could reach her long nose out and touch Bumpkins. The cat was still for a moment before he stretched out a paw.

I held my breath, but he only patted her nose. They

were being nice to each other. Amazing? Yes, but there it was.

Miz C waited until Bumpkins pulled his paw back before hugging the cat closer. She muttered, "Thank you for saving him," in Trixie's general direction then hurried toward her house.

I watched until woman and cat were inside, then held my hand out to Trixie, palm up. She high-fived me, and we turned toward our front door.

Chapter 24

A week later, we gathered in Ace's backyard to relax and catch up with our friends.

"Only in Ugly Creek." Steve shook his head. "First a dog napping FBI agent then my most trusted security person gets tangled up with a friend's wife who manipulates him into stealing secret government materials to get back at me for some sort of leftover high school jealousy thing."

Terri leaned back in the deck chair and stretched her legs out in front of her. Her newly adopted white-and-yellow kitten named Scrappy slept curled in her lap. "Sounds like the plot of a novel."

I laughed. "You're not wrong."

The breeze was cool, or at least to my thin Florida blood it was, but it was wonderful to be outside in the company of good friends. Dusty ran over, but instead of climbing into my lap as usual, she curled up under Terri's chair. I'd be jealous if the little critter wasn't so damn cute.

"It does sound like the plot for a novel, but I like the books I read to have happy endings." Stephie smiled at Jake.

"Me too," Liza said.

"I'm hoping for a happy ending tonight," Ace said, then whistled.

I was wondering what he was talking about, when

Hugh trotted around the corner of the house and sat in front of me. Behind his head, attached to his collar, was a small, square box.

I stared at Ace, who looked a little pale.

He smiled, though. "Open it."

I opened the box, and inside was a little blue velvet case designed to hold a ring. I worked hard at not hyperventilating, but my hand still shook as I opened it. The diamond ring was simple but beautiful, and tears filled my eyes. Then Ace was on one knee and both he and Hugh gave me big puppy eyes. "Would you consider marrying a rogue photojournalist who rescues dogs and regularly loses his cell phone?"

It was tempting to give him a hard time, but I figured we'd all been through enough. "Yes."

Ace reached out, but Hugh knocked him on his butt getting to me to lick my face. Ace shoved the huge dog out of the way and kissed me until I forgot everything except how much I loved this man.

Around us cheers, laughter, and barks filled the air. Doggone it, Ugly Creek really was the perfect place to start over.

A word about the author...

Cheryel Hutton is a Southern girl to the core. She was born in Tennessee and has spent most of her life there. Among the hills and valleys she found abundant inspiration for the stories she writes.

Recently she and her husband moved near Jacksonville, Florida, where they enjoy the sunshine, warm weather, and nearness to the ocean. Here Cheryel is discovering new inspiration and spends her time transcribing stories told to her by a muse who happens to be a dragon.

Cheryel has two other stories in her Ugly Creek series: *The Ugly Truth* and *Secrets of Ugly Creek*. She is also the author of *Blood of the Innocent* and *Keepers of Legend*.

You can find out more about Cheryel and Quill here:

www.cheryelhutton.com
www.dragonwhisperer.me

Thank you for purchasing
this publication of The Wild Rose Press, Inc.

If you enjoyed the story, we would appreciate your
letting others know by leaving a review.

For other wonderful stories,
please visit our on-line bookstore at
www.thewildrosepress.com.

For questions or more information
contact us at
info@thewildrosepress.com.

The Wild Rose Press, Inc.
www.thewildrosepress.com

Stay current with The Wild Rose Press, Inc.

Like us on Facebook

https://www.facebook.com/TheWildRosePress

And Follow us on Twitter
https://twitter.com/WildRosePress

www.ingramcontent.com/pod-product-compliance
Lightning Source LLC
Chambersburg PA
CBHW070338260626
47160CB00003B/1081